"What do I do? G

Sierra eased down ont[...]

As a second reporter's car parked in front, Taylor left the window. "I have an idea. Y'all can stay with my dad. He's a retired marine and loves children. Besides that, the holiday season is a big thing for my dad. It might help Ben to get away." He didn't know if it would, but his safety was the most important aspect to consider.

"We can't impose. We can keep the blinds closed. The press might get tired of waiting."

"First, you aren't imposing. I'll be there, too. Ben needs to be protected until we find the shooter. It didn't take long for the reporters to find where y'all were. The same can be said of the killer." Taylor sat next to Sierra on the sofa, so close a whiff of lavender teased his senses. "Let me call him and—"

A piercing scream reverberated through the house.

Margaret Daley, an award-winning author of ninety books (five million sold worldwide), has been married for over forty years and is a firm believer in romance and love. When she isn't traveling, she's writing love stories, often with a suspense thread, and corralling her three cats, who think they rule her household. To find out more about Margaret, visit her website at margaretdaley.com.

Visit the Author Profile page at Harlequin.com for more titles.

LONE STAR CHRISTMAS WITNESS

MARGARET DALEY

HARLEQUIN® LOVE INSPIRED® SUSPENSE

Recycling programs
for this product may
not exist in your area.

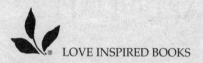

LOVE INSPIRED BOOKS

ISBN-13: 978-1-335-54417-9

Lone Star Christmas Witness

Copyright © 2018 by Margaret Daley

All rights reserved. Except for use in any review, the reproduction
or utilization of this work in whole or in part in any form by any
electronic, mechanical or other means, now known or hereafter
invented, including xerography, photocopying and recording, or in
any information storage or retrieval system, is forbidden without
the written permission of the editorial office, Love Inspired Books,
195 Broadway, New York, NY 10007 U.S.A.

This is a work of fiction. Names, characters, places and incidents are
either the product of the author's imagination or are used fictitiously, and
any resemblance to actual persons, living or dead, business establishments,
events or locales is entirely coincidental.

This edition published by arrangement with Love Inspired Books.

® and TM are trademarks of Love Inspired Books, used under license.
Trademarks indicated with ® are registered in the United States Patent
and Trademark Office, the Canadian Intellectual Property Office and in
other countries.

www.Harlequin.com

Printed in U.S.A.

The Lord is my light and my salvation; whom shall I fear?
The Lord is the strength of my life;
of whom shall I be afraid?
—*Psalms* 27:1

ONE

Texas Ranger Taylor Blackburn strode toward the clinic, ducking under the crime scene tape. A northwest wind blew, a chill in the winter air. Dread threatened to slow his pace, but he couldn't allow that. Forty-five minutes ago, a woman reported a shooting—a madman had entered this building right before it opened and shot the six employees on the staff. Five were dead, one critically injured.

When Taylor entered the Premier Medical Clinic, the smell of copper and gunpowder accosted him. Sadly, he'd smelled those aromas too many times in his sixteen years in law enforcement. His gaze swept the reception area, pausing for a few seconds on the downed pine tree with its multicolored tiny lights twinkling among the green foliage and the many ornaments lying on the floor. Tangled in the midst of the tree lay the first victim, a middle-aged woman dressed in her nurse's scrubs—the vision making a mockery of what Christmas stood for.

Lieutenant Nash Cartwright with the San Antonio Police Department approached Taylor, who had been called in because it was a mass shooting. "It's good to see you."

Taylor shook his hand, glad that Nash was the SAPD's lead on this case. He'd worked with the lieutenant several times. "I wish under different circumstances."

"Me, too. We don't know much yet. An unidentified man moved methodically through the building taking out the cameras as he went and killing anyone in his path. From what little we saw on the surveillance footage before it went black, the gun had a silencer on it."

"There wasn't anything that could identify the suspect?"

"He knew where the cameras were and made sure we didn't see his face even during the brief time he was caught on tape. All we know is he's approximately six feet tall with a slender build. His clothing was all black, with a hoodie to hide his face. Nothing else."

"Was the door unlocked?" Taylor glanced at the security system pad near the front door.

"Don't know. The alarm was off when we arrived."

Taylor had briefly noticed a rear parking lot, most likely where the employees parked, which probably meant there was another entrance there. "Even with a silencer, you can hear the muffled shots. But no one escaped the building out the back door?"

"Right. It was blocked by a big trash bin. One male doctor was killed trying to leave."

Taylor glanced down the hallway and saw another body by the exit, the door opened partially but a large garbage bin against the wall on the outside. "So, the killer came in and left by the front entrance. Any surveillance cameras outside in the parking lots in the back or front?"

"Yes, but taken down beforehand. I just sent some officers out to canvass the other businesses on the street, but with this clinic set back from the road and not surrounded by close neighbors, we might not get anything. And there are no traffic cams on this side street that could show us cars turning into the clinic. We'll look later at other traffic cams in the general area during the time frame and try to identify the license numbers."

"Who reported this shooting?"

"The first patient of the day, at eight. An older woman—Gladys Mills. She's outside in a car with a female officer. She was shaken up and could only tell us she didn't see anyone leaving the building or hanging around."

Its location had made this place an easier target, Taylor knew. But he wondered whether this attack was random or targeted. "Any drugs taken?"

Nash frowned. "No. The drugs were locked up, and there are no signs the locks were tampered with, so we can rule that angle out."

Taylor moved down the hall to the man by the rear door, dressed in a white coat. He stooped and examined the body, facedown, with an entry bullet hole in his back. "The only doctor here?"

"No, Dr. Noah Porter runs the clinic with one other doctor—a female, Dr. Kathleen Markham."

"Is she one of the dead victims?"

"Yes. She was still in her office." Nash gestured to a shorter corridor off the main one. "At the end."

The door was open, but from this view Taylor couldn't see the victim. "Are all the employees here today? Most clinics, even small ones, have more than six employees."

"No. There are two not here if the information we've dug up is right. One is a male nurse, Colin Brewer, and the other is Sierra Walker, who manages the clinic. I have two officers tracking down the missing employees."

"Good." It was possible one of them or both were involved in the shooting or at the very least might have information that could help this investigation. "I especially want to talk to the office manager. This could have been done by a disgruntled employee—past or present. Knowing why will help us find this guy. Where are the other two dead victims?"

"There." Nash pointed to the counter in the middle of the building where the nurses probably worked.

Taylor walked around a large booth to find two women on the tiled floor—one shot in the back, the other in the chest. From what he had seen so far, the shooter was swift and accurate—possibly methodical in his execution of the crime, as though he'd planned it for a while.

Nash received a call. His frown deepened the longer he listened to the caller. When it ended, he took a few seconds to gather himself, then said, "The sixth victim died on the way to the hospital. She never regained consciousness. Mindy Carson worked the front desk where she was found alive." He started to walk away, then turned back to Taylor. "Look around. I'll be in the lobby."

As Taylor walked toward the female doctor's office, he couldn't shake his bad feeling, a growing hollowness in his gut. If this wasn't a current or former disgruntled employee, then what drove a person to kill all these people who were healers trying to help others get well? The shooter hadn't come in while patients were here. He'd done this before they opened the clinic. This wasn't a random choice. The shooter wanted one or all of these people dead.

He stepped into Dr. Markham's office, noting the lock on the door had been shot out, and paused a few feet inside, scanning the medium-sized room. A woman in her thirties, wearing a white coat, lay on the floor near a bank of windows that didn't open. Trapped in her office with no way out. He covered the distance to the doctor, who lay faceup, an entry wound to her heart. She hadn't suffered at least.

As he gazed at a face caught in a look of terror, he whispered, "Who wanted you dead?" He wished the victim could tell him.

The sound of faint whimpers wafted to Taylor. He stiffened and whirled around, every part of him on alert. But the room was empty. His gaze swept more carefully over the office, stopping at a framed picture on Dr. Markham's desk of her and a little boy.

Did he imagine the noise?

Again, he surveyed the area, looking for any place to hide. The only furniture was a desk with two chairs in front and one behind, as well as a sideboard along the opposite wall with more photos of the doctor and the boy with a few including another woman. He strode over to the piece of furniture for a closer look. The sideboard had drawers down the middle, and cabinets on the sides with louvered doors. He opened the nearest cupboard. Files, books and magazines were crammed inside. He moved to the other one on the left and swung the door wide.

A child was curled into a tight ball, his head buried against his knees. Another whimper escaped the kid's mouth as he tried to crouch even more into a protective cocoon.

Taylor squatted in front of the child. "You're safe. I'm Texas Ranger Blackburn, and I won't let anything happen to you." A lance pierced his heart as he waited for the boy to trust him. Finally, the child looked up, and Taylor recognized him as the boy from the photographs. Dr. Markham's son probably. He could only imagine the horror this young child went through when the killer came into the office. Did he see or hear anything through the slats in the cabinet door?

Taylor wondered who the other woman in a couple of the photographs was. She looked like Dr. Markham. She looked too old to be her child. A sister maybe?

"No one is going to hurt you. I promise. You're safe." Taylor held out his hand.

The brown-haired child didn't move.

Taylor withdrew his cell phone and called Nash rather than leave the child alone to find the lieutenant. "Will you send a police officer to find Kathleen Markham's residence and see if there's a family member there?"

"Why?"

"I found Dr. Markham's son in her office."

"Alive?"

"Yes." As Taylor disconnected, he held out his hand again toward the child. "Come on out. You're safe."

But the kid quickly turned his face away from Taylor.

He settled himself on the floor by the child. He didn't want him to feel he was alone nor did he want to force him out of the cabinet. Taylor glanced up at the photo of Dr. Markham, the boy and a young woman who had long blond hair and a smile that lit her whole face. She had her arm around the kid, looking down at him. Suddenly a thought struck him. What if the boy was this lady's son, not Dr. Markham's?

Sierra Walker left the Premier Medical Clinic's accountant's office, relieved to get the necessary paperwork to him for the end of the year. She hurried toward her car, the cold wind whipping her long blond hair about her face and sending a shiver down her spine. Reaching her Mustang, she opened the driver's side door and slipped behind the steering wheel.

She hoped Kat could figure out what was wrong with Ben. Probably a cold or possibly the flu. After her nephew had spent yesterday at the clinic, sleeping most of the time in one of the exam rooms, Sierra had told her sister that she'd take Ben with her today and work at home when she finished meeting with the accountant.

When she turned onto the street that led to work, the sight of police cruisers parked along the street in front of the clinic with lights flashing sent terror snaking down her spine. A small crowd stood behind a makeshift barricade.

She parked along the street, then dug her cell phone out of her purse. Her hands shook as she called her sister, her full attention glued to the police going in and out of the building. When Kat didn't answer, she stuffed her phone back into her handbag and scrambled from her car.

Her pace, matching her pounding heartbeat, quickened with each step she took toward the barricade. She fought her way through the throng, praying everyone was all right, especially Kat and Ben. They were her only family. Her sister was the one who rescued her when she started down the wrong path. She owed her so much.

She reached the cordoned-off area and ducked under the barrier. A police officer immediately confronted her. "Ma'am, you aren't supposed to be here. Please stay behind the barricade."

"I work here. What happened? Is everyone all right?"

"Who are you?"

"Sierra Walker. I'm the office manager, and my sister, Dr. Markham, works here, too."

"Can I see some identification?"

With trembling hands Sierra dug into her purse and presented her wallet with her driver's license.

"Come this way."

As she walked beside the officer, she scanned the scene and realized that something really bad had happened for this kind of all-out response and interest from bystanders. The nearer she came to the entrance, the more distress wrapped around her and squeezed the breath from her lungs, making her chest hurt.

The officer stopped while a gurney with a closed body bag was wheeled from the building.

"Please tell me if my sister and her son are okay." She didn't know how the words passed her tight throat.

He didn't answer but continued to make his way into the clinic as the gurney was rolled toward a waiting vehicle. Sweat popped out on Sierra's forehead in spite of the cold weather. The stench assailed her senses as she moved farther inside. Her stomach roiled.

When the sight of a body's shape taped on the bloodstained floor by the Christmas tree across from the receptionist's desk transfixed Sierra, she stopped as though frozen in place. Who was dead? Mindy, the receptionist? Mindy was one of her best friends. They often shared lunch here at the clinic or the café across the street. Then Sierra thought of all the other people she worked with who could be on that gurney, and her heart broke into pieces.

The officer glanced back. "I'm taking you to someone who can answer your questions."

She heard the words he said, but they seemed to come to her as if she were in a long tunnel and he was at the other end.

"Ma'am, are you okay?"

Sierra closed her eyes for a few seconds, and when she opened them again, a man over six feet tall, dressed in a long-sleeve white shirt, with a blue tie, an off-white cowboy hat and tan pants, headed toward her. Her focus latched onto the circular star badge he wore slightly to the left, over his heart. A Texas Ranger—which usually meant not a routine crime.

The Texas Ranger with deep green eyes and dark brown hair held out his arm. "Sierra Walker?"

She shook his hand. "Yes. What has happened here?" Her voice quavered, and she swallowed hard, trying to prepare herself for the worst—Mindy was in the body bag.

"There's no good way to say this. A shooter came to the clinic right before it opened and shot everyone who was here. Is Dr. Kathleen Markham your sister? That's what the officer said."

Fear froze her lungs. "Yes. Is she hurt bad?" *Please don't let her be the person in the body bag.*

"I'm Texas Ranger Taylor Blackburn. Let's go in here." He motioned toward a room behind the receptionist desk.

Part of the area was partitioned for her workplace. "My office is back there." Moving forward, Sierra made the mistake of glancing down the main hallway, and when her eyes lit on a male body by the back door, she stumbled.

A hand grasped her arm, and the Texas Ranger stopped her from falling. Heat flushed her cheeks. "I wasn't expecting that. Who is it? Dr. Porter?"

He looked down at her. "Yes, it's him."

She stared into those green eyes, and in that moment, she knew no one survived the mass shooting. Kathleen! Ben! Mindy and the others. Tears sprang into her eyes and blurred her vision. "Is my sister's body still here?"

"No. It was the first one removed. Let's go to your office." He gestured to the room filled with file cabinets.

Sierra nodded. As she made her way there, she averted her face and wiped the wet tracks from her cheeks. She couldn't even bring herself to ask about Ben. She'd helped raise her seven-year-old nephew since he was born, especially while Kathleen was a resident with long hours then when she started the clinic. For his first few years, Sierra's life had revolved around him.

As Texas Ranger Blackburn closed the door, she leaned against her desk to help support her. A huge lump clogged her throat, and she gulped—several times—before she felt she could ask him the question she'd never thought she would say. "My nephew, Ben, was here with his mom. Is he—"

The Texas Ranger closed the space between them, his green eyes softening. "Ben is the only person who survived."

At first, she thought she hadn't heard correctly. She started to question him, but his look of compassion gave her hope. "How?"

"He hid in a cupboard in your sister's office. Most likely the shooter didn't know he was there."

Opposite emotions—happiness for Ben and a deep sadness for Kat—assailed her. She shut her eyes and tried to compose her thoughts. "Where is he? Can I see him?"

"Soon. First, you and I need to talk."

"But he has to be frightened. What has he said?"

"Nothing. Since I took him from the cupboard, he hasn't cried or said anything."

"He's in shock."

"Yes, and we have someone with him right now." He gestured toward a chair nearby. "Sit. Let's talk. The child psychologist I called will be through soon."

Everything around Sierra vanished, and all she saw was the law enforcement officer, taking a seat across from her. How had she ended up sitting down? She didn't even remember doing that. She had to be dreaming. Any moment she would wake up and see Kathleen and Ben.

"Ms. Walker, are you okay?" Concern laced the Texas Ranger's deep voice.

She blinked, and reality zoomed into focus. "No. What do you want to ask me? I want to be with Ben as soon as possible. He has to feel…" *As numb and lost as I am?*

"Were you at the clinic at any time this morning?"

"No. I left our house and went right to an eight o'clock meeting with the clinic's accounting firm. The meeting was over at ten thirty, and I came straight here."

"What's the name of the accounting firm?"

For a few seconds, she became defensive, her hands curling into a ball. How in the world could he think she might have something to do with the killings? She cared for everyone at the clinic, especially Mindy, and her sister had been more like a mother to her since their mom died when Sierra was twelve.

"Jones Smith Accounting. We've been a client for the past five years. Zachery Jones was the partner I met with this morning. He'll verify I was there between eight and ten thirty."

The Texas Ranger wrote down the information she gave him, then glanced up.

She rose partway. "Now can I see Ben?"

"I know this is hard, but I have a few more questions. Have there been any threats against the clinic or one of the employees recently?"

She sat back down, trying to remember, but her mind felt as though it were on overload. She shook her head. "I don't think…" Something nagged at her, but the thought stayed at the back of her mind, vague and muddy.

"What is it?" the Texas Ranger prompted.

She tried to focus, rubbing her forehead, and then she recalled. "It was last summer. There was a father who blamed Dr. Porter for his daughter's death, but he was grieving at the sudden turn of events. Dr. Porter did everything he could."

"Who?"

"I'd have to look back through the files."

"Anyone else?"

"Another patient was mad because he was

still in pain and wanted more medication. My sister wouldn't write a prescription. She's especially careful about that because of the opiate crisis. That situation happened last month. The guy's name was Bruce Lockhart." Tension pounded against her temples. Her nerves were stretched so tight she wondered if they would snap in two. "I can't think of anyone else right now. I need to look through the appointment log and possibly the records. But even then, I might not be able to come up with more. I work all day in here, and don't have a lot to do with the patients. Something could have happened, and I might not know about it." She paused. "Although Mindy usually kept me informed, even about the employees' personal life, but nothing to warrant this."

"Are the doors to the clinic kept locked until it opens?"

"Yes. It gives the staff time to meet if needed."

"Who has a key to the building?"

"I do. Also my sister, Dr. Porter and Colin Brewer. He's a nurse and he's been here from the beginning. Everyone who has a key also has the alarm system code. After the employees who don't have a key arrive, the front door is locked until it's time to open."

He wrote down the names, the lines on his face deepening. "Where is Ben's father?"

When Sierra thought about Kalvin and what he'd done, she couldn't help but frown. "He left Kathleen a few months after Ben was born. He gave her full custody and walked away. He's never contacted her. The last she knew he was overseas. That was a couple of years ago."

"What does he do?"

"I don't know. He was in security. That's what he called it."

"What is Ben's father's name?"

"Kalvin Markham."

"When you say overseas, where?"

"The Middle East. I got the impression he moved around a lot." Sierra massaged her temples, trying to rid her head of the increasing pain.

"What kind of arrangements did your sister have for Ben if anything happened to her?"

The conversation she and Kathleen had several years ago flooded her thoughts. She hadn't wanted to discuss the issue, but her older sister had insisted. Kat had been practical about things while Sierra had wanted to avoid the what-ifs. She'd learned to live for the moment, although with her job and her part in Ben's life that had been changing.

"I'm Ben's guardian if anything happened to Kathleen. She has a will leaving everything to her son, with me being the executor of her will and his trustee until Ben turns twenty-one. She wanted to make sure Kalvin could never get ahold of her money, especially now that she was an established doctor."

"How long has this clinic been open?"

"Five years." She was done answering questions. She needed to see for herself that Ben was alive. She needed to hold him. "I'm sorry, but right now, I want to see my nephew. I don't want him to think something happened to me, too."

"Yes, I understand. We can continue this conversation later. I have some information to help me proceed with the investigation. I'll be working with the SAPD on this case." He rose. "The child psychologist should be through talking to Ben by now."

Sierra grasped the arms of the chair and pushed herself to a standing position, her legs feeling as though she'd just finished a marathon run carrying twenty-pound weights. Following the Texas Ranger from her office, she kept her eyes forward, doing her best to avoid looking at Dr. Porter's body. She was thankful two officers were blocking her view this time.

Texas Ranger Blackburn clasped the knob to

one of the exam rooms. "Ben's in here, and I would like him to remain here until all the bodies are removed. Dr. Porter is the last one. The child psychologist is Dr. John Yates."

How did this officer deal with something like what happened at the clinic and remain so composed? She wanted to fall apart and cry until there was nothing left in her. But for Ben's sake, she couldn't.

She walked into the exam room first, immediately seeing her nephew huddled into a ball, his head buried against his knees. Her broken heart further shattered into thousands of pieces. She hurried to his side and placed her hand on his hunched back. "Ben, I'm here. You aren't alone."

Nothing.

She stroked his back, something she did when he was upset. "Ben, we'll be able to leave here in a few minutes."

Still not a word.

She glanced over her shoulder at the child psychologist. He signaled he wanted to talk with her outside in the hall. "I love you, Ben. I'll be right back."

She stepped outside with the man while the Texas Ranger stayed in the exam room. "Did he say anything to you?"

Dr. Yates shook his head. "No. Not one word. I was with him forty-five minutes. When he's upset, does he refuse to talk?"

"Never. He can talk your ear off. What does this mean?"

"It's possible he has traumatic muteness."

"Will he ever talk again?"

"Hopefully. But he's witnessed a horrific crime," Dr. Yates said. "He was hiding in a cabinet. Your sister most likely put him there and told him not to say a word."

Sierra paced toward the reception area, spied the bloodstain on the floor and turned back around. "What can we do, Dr. Yates? We've got to help him."

"Please call me John. I would like to work with him."

"Yes, anything to help him cope with this." She couldn't imagine what her nephew was going through. She was an adult, and she was struggling to deal with what happened to Kat.

"For the first couple of sessions, I'd like to come to his house. I'm hoping a familiar place will help him. I will tell you he didn't curl up into a ball until Taylor left the room to talk to you."

"Have you worked with Texas Ranger Blackburn before?"

"Yes, whenever a child is involved in a case. Now, if it's all right with you, I'd like to have our first session today. From what Taylor told me, Ben's the only one who might have seen or heard something that could help the case. In fact, perhaps it would be best if Taylor was at the session, too."

"Anything you think will help Ben and find the killer. Holding it inside only makes the situation worse." She'd found that out the hard way when as teenager she'd kept a secret that ate at her soul until she finally turned to the Lord with her sister's help. Kat was the only other person who knew about it.

"Good." John swung around and opened the door to the exam room.

When she went inside, Ben sat on the edge of the exam bed, his legs hanging down. His chin rested on his chest, but he wasn't in a ball like before. Taylor Blackburn leaned against the piece of furniture next to Ben as if he was in deep thought.

"Ben, I want to take you home. I don't know about you, but I'm getting hungry. We can stop and get some hamburgers at your favorite place. Okay?"

Her nephew lifted his head and nodded once, then returned his stare to the floor.

For a moment, panic set in. She wasn't prepared to take her sister's place and become Ben's full-time caregiver. *What if I make a mistake? Lord, I need help. Where do I start?*

She kept her focus on God, and slowly calmness overtook the anxiousness. Sierra held out her hand. "Let's go home."

Ben took it and slid off the exam table, the whole time still staring at the floor. At the door, her nephew spun around and threw himself at Taylor, clinging to him. The Texas Ranger's eyes widened, connecting with hers. Ben's reaction confirmed what Dr. Yates had pointed out, that Taylor had a calming effect on her nephew. That made sense to her. In Ben's eyes, Taylor had saved him when he found him hiding in Kat's office.

She clasped one of Ben's shoulders. "Let's go home."

Her nephew released his hold and stepped away from Taylor with hesitation. Ben took Sierra's hand but kept his gaze on Taylor. What was she supposed to do? She tried to remember what she'd felt when her mother died.

She headed toward the front exit, trying her best to block Ben's view of the bloodstains on the reception floor. As she reached to pull the door open, Taylor and John appeared right behind them.

"We'll follow you to your house," Taylor said as he opened the door for them and they left the clinic.

Relief blanketed her. "Thanks."

In the short time she had been inside, the crowd outside had doubled, and more media had arrived. She hadn't thought about that. She didn't want to talk to a reporter, nor did she want Ben to be questioned by them.

As they neared the barricades, Taylor came around her. "I'll take the lead. You don't have to talk to the press. In fact, I'd recommend you don't."

"I'm not going to." The eagerness she glimpsed on the reporters' faces made her feel as though she was the prey and they were waiting to devour her to get their story.

"Where's your car?"

"It's the red Mustang to the right down the street."

"Good. It's not that far from my SUV."

Two police officers moved the barricade, so they could leave. As they plunged into the crowd, Sierra and Ben were immediately surrounded by reporters shouting questions at them, a lot of them holding microphones while cameramen angled for a good shot of her and her nephew. Panic shot through her at the thought the whole world would see their picture on the news—and realize Ben survived the attack.

As she dodged the media, she wondered how in the world she was going to protect Ben from his memories of today—and from the killer.

TWO

Taylor pulled in behind Sierra's car that she'd driven into the garage, while Dr. Yates parked along the curb. On his trip here, Taylor had checked Sierra's alibi and the accounting firm had confirmed her presence and the time she left that morning. He hadn't thought she was the killer, but he'd learned to check every lead out.

In fact, the interviews with both of them had been difficult for him, especially Ben's. The little boy with brown hair and eyes reminded him of his deceased son. TJ had died from cancer at the age of six over three years ago. He'd left a hole in Taylor's heart that he'd never been able to fill. Months after his son's death, Taylor had been accepted as a Texas Ranger after serving as a Texas State Trooper. He'd thrown himself into the job as though that would cover the pain of his loss. It hadn't. That was why he preferred working from behind a computer rather than in the field. At least until a few months ago. Working a case with Texas Ranger Dallas Sanders involving kidnapped babies had made him realize he couldn't hide forever.

When he realized he was gripping the steering wheel so hard pain shot up his arms, he pried his fingers loose and slid from his vehicle. He bridged the distance to Sierra, holding her car door open while Ben slowly crawled from the back seat. As he straightened, Ben glanced up at Taylor. The look of terror in the child's eyes reminded him of when TJ had gone for his first chemo treatment. Taylor hadn't been able to protect his son then. He intended to protect Ben now. He wasn't helpless in this situation. He'd find the murderer.

When John Yates joined them, Sierra put the garage door down and walked with her hand on Ben's shoulder to the porch of the two-story, adobe-styled home. Taylor hung back and surveyed the surroundings. No one had followed them to the house, but it wouldn't have been hard for the killer to figure out where Dr. Markham lived with her sister and son. There was still a possibility the shooting was random, but more likely it wasn't. So, what motivated the person to kill six people? If he could answer that, it would be a lot easier to find the shooter.

Taylor was the last one to enter the Markham home. He locked the door behind him and faced Sierra across the foyer. Her long, curly strawberry blond hair reminded him of a setting sun striking the mountains in Big Bend National Park. But what really drew his attention were her big brown eyes with long, dark eyelashes, filled with pain from losing a loved one. That look drew him. In the past nine years, he'd gone through the same kind of sorrow twice. He felt a connection with her, which surprised him because he worked hard to keep himself walled off. He couldn't deal with that kind of pain for a third time.

Sierra tore her gaze away from his. "We should go into the kitchen." She led the way down a hall, and when she entered the room, she gestured toward the table in a nook with a bay window overlooking the fenced backyard. While they were all settled except her, she asked, "What would you like to drink? We have sweet tea, water and milk, but if you would like coffee, I can make some."

"Sweet tea is fine for me," Taylor said while John nodded. He rose and strolled to the counter next to the refrigerator as Sierra opened the door. "Here, let me help you. Where are the glasses?"

"The cabinet in front of you." Her hand shaking, she immediately set the pitcher on the ceramic tiles.

Taylor leaned close to her. "You have enough to do. The least I can do is take care of this. Go sit down."

"Thanks."

He quickly filled the glasses, set them on the table and returned the pitcher to the refrigerator. When he took his seat between Ben and John, he looked up into Sierra's brown eyes across the table, glimpsing a sadness he was all too familiar with.

After John finished chewing a bite of his hamburger, he said, "Ben, this is fantastic. Now I see why this is your favorite place to get a burger."

The boy kept his head down while eating his food.

Taylor fixed his attention on Ben. "Dr. Yates, I agree with you. This is great."

The child slid his glance to Taylor for a fleeting few seconds.

John nodded at Taylor, a signal they had talked about earlier. If Ben wasn't responding to John, his friend wanted Taylor to ask a few questions and see what response he could get from the traumatized boy.

Over the years Taylor had interviewed a lot

of victims and witnesses, but in this case, he felt the weight of what he was doing. He wasn't a child psychologist, but at least John was here to guide him.

"Ben, sometimes when I'm upset, I can't explain things well. That's normal. I noticed some pictures on the refrigerator. Are those yours? Do you like to draw?"

The young boy turned his head slightly toward Taylor, then went back to eating.

"Ben draws a lot, as you can see." Sierra pointed toward the fridge. "He has an area in his room where he has paper, pencils, markers and other items for a budding artist."

"That's great, Ben. Maybe after lunch, you can show me your room."

He nodded but didn't look at Taylor.

Ten minutes later Ben and Sierra headed upstairs with Taylor behind them. John was waiting a moment before following. When Taylor entered the bedroom, the sight of a large corkboard with a ton of drawings pinned to it sent relief through him. According to John, some kids expressed their emotions through their artwork. He remembered in the baby kidnapping case how Michelle Sanders, the daughter of Dallas Sanders, a fellow Texas Ranger and friend, and the thirteen-year-old babysitter of the first child abducted, had helped their case and had been pivotal in solving the crime.

"You're quite an artist, Ben. I'd love for you to draw a picture for me," Taylor said.

Ben sat down at his table but didn't do anything except stare at a blank sheet. Taylor and Sierra hovered over the child, not sure what else to do. When John appeared in the doorway, Ben finally picked up a black marker and scribbled all over the paper. Then he snapped up the picture and wadded it into a tight ball. Tears ran down his face as he threw it at the wall. Hanging his head, he hunched his shoulders.

Sierra squatted next to her nephew, putting her arm around him. "Sweetie, I'm here for you." She gave him a hug, tears glistening in her eyes. "Can you tell us anything about this morning?"

Silence.

Taylor knelt on the other side of the boy. "You're safe. I'm not going to let anything happen to you. Remember, I promised."

After five long minutes, when Ben didn't say anything or make any kind of movement to indicate he'd even heard him, Taylor glanced over his shoulder at John, who motioned for Taylor to come into the hallway. He rose and took a step away. Suddenly Ben shot up, his chair tumbling backward, and threw his arms around Taylor as though to stop him from leaving.

Still he spoke not a word.

Taylor clasped the boy, not sure what he should do.

Sierra came to Ben's side. "Hon, it's okay if you don't want to draw. Texas Ranger Blackburn was only going out into the hallway to talk with Dr. Yates. You need to let him do that."

"Ben, I'll be right back."

The child let go and immediately clung to his aunt.

As Taylor left the bedroom, he heard Sierra say, "You won't be alone. You're safe now."

He hoped so for the child's sake.

Taylor joined John in the hall, and they moved away from the doorway. "What do we do?"

"Ben needs to feel safe. After the kind of trauma he went through, he's frightened, possibly wondering when the person will come back and get him. He took his anger and fear out on the paper."

Taylor frowned, remembering the young boy crammed into a cabinet, probably told not to say a word. "I can't imagine the horror he went through when he witnessed his mother being murdered. He could have seen the whole thing through the slats in the cupboard door. At the very least, he heard it. I was hoping he would tell us what he saw and heard. We don't have a lot to go on right now. What should we do?"

"We?"

"How can I turn my back on the boy?" *And Sierra.*

"I see the resemblance of Ben to TJ. Is that why you feel you need to go above and beyond your job?"

John had helped TJ deal with his leukemia and then even helped Taylor deal with TJ's death. "Don't bring my son into this. Ben isn't TJ. I know that. But he's a scared child and the only witness to the shooting."

"Are you being honest with yourself?"

"I'm going to make sure he's safe. What if the man comes after Ben because he thinks the child saw him?"

"How are you going to do that?"

"I don't know yet, but I'll figure out something. If anything happens to Ben, I'd never forgive myself."

"Like TJ?"

Taylor balled his hands. "I did everything I could to save my son. And I'll do the same for Ben." The memory of the boy clinging to him when he rescued Ben from the cabinet wasn't something he would forget anytime soon.

John stepped closer and lowered his voice. "I know. But don't mix the two up. Ben needs to feel safe. His view of the world has been shattered today. And there's a chance he'll never remember the details of what happened or even talk again. Our mind sometimes will suppress a tragic incident in order to cope with what happened." He looked over at the door to Ben's room. "That doesn't mean it won't affect the boy on a subconscious level."

A sound to Taylor's left brought him around to face Sierra as she came into the hallway. Grief had carved lines into her features, darkened her eyes. "How's Ben?"

"He's asleep right now."

"That doesn't surprise me. Intense emotions are exhausting." All Taylor had wanted to do when TJ had died was retreat from life and sleep.

Sierra's mouth thinned into a tight line. "I want to find who did this."

"And I don't want Ben to overhear this conversation." John turned toward the stairs. "Why don't we go downstairs and discuss what needs to be done in the days to come."

Taylor followed behind Sierra, descending the steps and crossing to the living room. In front of the large window stood a Christmas tree, laden with tiny white lights, red garland and dozens of ornaments, a lot of them appearing homemade. He felt as though he'd stepped into a Christmas store. Since his son died, he hadn't even put up a tree.

Sierra took a seat on the couch at one end while he sat in a chair across from her. John joined her on the couch. For a long moment silence ruled.

John cleared his throat. "For the next few days, I'd like to visit with Ben here at this house. This is where he's felt safe and secure. I'm hoping that will help him begin to bring down his walls."

Sierra folded her hands together in her lap as she faced the doctor. "I'm concerned. He hasn't said a word so far. And like I said, Ben is a talkative child. He never goes long without talking."

"Selective mutism is often caused by trauma. If we can deal with the cause, he'll hopefully begin to talk again. But if he does, that doesn't mean he'll pour out the details of what happened this morning. I want to give him techniques to deal with stress and trauma. I think one of the best ways for him will be through his art. He's very good at drawing for his age. He may never be able to say what happened with words, but maybe he will in pictures."

Taylor remembered the myriad illustrations plastered all over the large corkboard in Ben's bedroom, not to mention some in frames hanging on the walls. He wondered if Michelle Sanders could help Ben get started. The teenager had a way with children and certainly knew about being involved in a traumatic situation. Two people had kidnapped her nephew while she had been babysitting him and had left her injured. He'd call her father, Dallas, and see what he thought about it.

"What should I do to help?" Sierra asked John, twisting her hands together while chewing on her bottom lip.

"Love him. Keep his routine as normal as possible. And make sure he feels safe." John stood and gave her a business card. "Call me at any time if you need me. I'll be back tomorrow at eight before I go in for my first appointment."

"I'll walk you out." Taylor pushed to his feet and accompanied John into the foyer. At the front door he finally said, "Thanks for coming on such short notice. I didn't know what to do at the clinic. He wouldn't let go of me."

"Anytime. We've been friends for a long time." He shook Taylor's hand. "You know, there's a chance we'll never know what happened from Ben."

"But the killer doesn't know that. That's what I'm worried about."

"Ben's in good hands with you."

As John left, a news van pulled up to the curb in front of the house. While Taylor gripped the edge of the door, a cameraman and woman reporter climbed from their vehicle and started for the porch. He immediately stepped outside and met the pair on the sidewalk leading to Sierra's home.

"We understand Ben Markham was the only surviving person at the clinic. Has he said anything about the shooting? What does the killer look like? Can the boy identify him?"

Although the police had withheld Ben's name, he'd known it wouldn't take the press long to figure it out, and now the killer would know for sure there was a potential witness. In addition to working the case, now he needed to find a place to keep Ben safe from the media and possibly the shooter.

He threw his shoulders back in an imposing gesture as he made a statement. "The families of the victims are dealing with a difficult situation. Please respect their privacy and grief. The police department will be giving a statement later today. Do not trespass on this property, or I'll arrest you."

He spun around and marched to the porch while the reporter asked, "Why wasn't Sierra Walker at the clinic? She's the office manager."

He felt the urge to slam the front door but refrained. He didn't want to alarm Ben in any way. So he closed it quietly.

Sierra stood in the foyer with her arms folded over her chest. "I don't want them to upset Ben any more than he already is. Are they leaving?"

Taylor headed into the living room and stared out the large front window. "No. They're standing by their van. There'll be more before the day is over." He turned toward Sierra.

The ashen cast to her face highlighted her large, dark brown eyes. "No! They can't. Ben will see them. They will scare him even more."

"As long as they stay off your property, there's little I can do except find you and Ben another place to stay for the time being. A place that the reporters don't know about."

Sierra eased down onto the couch. "Like what? A hotel?"

As a second car parked in front, Taylor left the window. "I have an idea. Y'all can stay with my dad. He lives in a small town right outside of San Antonio. He's a retired Marine and loves children. My sister, who lives three hours away, has a nine-year-old daughter and a five-year-old son. Besides that, the holiday season is a big thing for my dad. It might help Ben to get away." He didn't know if it would, but the boy's safety was the most important aspect to consider.

"We can't impose. We can keep the blinds closed. The press might get tired of waiting."

"First, you aren't imposing. I know my dad. He would be the first to tell you to come to his place. I'll be there, too. I think Ben needs to be protected until we find the shooter. It didn't take long for the reporters to find where y'all were. The same can be said of the killer." Taylor sat next to her on the sofa, so close a whiff of vanilla teased his senses. "Let me call him and—"

A piercing scream reverberated through the house.

THREE

The shrill sound from the second floor chilled Sierra to her core. She jumped up at the same time as Taylor surged to his feet and raced toward the staircase, withdrawing his gun. He took the steps two at a time while she followed closely behind him. He disappeared inside Ben's room a few feet before her. When she entered, she nearly ran into Taylor, poised in the entrance with his gun raised.

Sierra peered around him, her heartbeat racing. "Where's Ben?"

He shifted his attention from one area of the bedroom to the next, lingering on the window. He walked to it and checked to see if it was locked. "I don't know."

While Taylor stooped down and inspected beneath the bed, Sierra went to look in the bathroom, knowing of two places Ben had used when they'd played hide-and-seek. But

Ben wasn't between the stool and counter or in the bathtub.

As she reentered the bedroom, Taylor opened the closet door. Ben sat hunched over, covering his ears. When her nephew dropped his hands to his sides and looked up, his tear-soaked face ripped at her composure.

Being closer, Taylor holstered his weapon and squatted next to Ben. "You must have had a bad dream. You're safe. I'm not going to let anyone hurt you." Slowly he reached out and laid his hand on her nephew's back.

Sierra knelt next to Taylor. "And neither am I." Earlier she'd wanted to stay at this house because Ben was familiar with his surroundings, but with the press outside, she knew that wasn't possible. Their presence would be a constant reminder to Ben and her of what had happened today. "You aren't alone, sweetie."

Taylor pulled back to allow her to slide her arm along Ben's shoulders. The boy turned his head, looked at her with red eyes, then lunged toward her and pressed against her. She hugged him, listening to the sobs pouring out of him.

Today had forever changed Ben's life—and hers. Would he ever be able to deal with the trauma of this morning? Would he ever talk again?

Taylor leaned close to Sierra's ear and whispered, "I'm going to call my dad."

As he rose, Ben reached out and clutched Taylor's arm.

"I'll be right back," he told the boy. "I'm not leaving the house. I'm here for you."

Slowly her nephew let go of Taylor. Ben leaned against Sierra and watched him exit the bedroom.

"Honey, you're his number one priority." Should she say anything about leaving the house? What if Taylor's dad didn't want them to come to his place? She'd wait until the plans were finalized. Ben needed stability. Not being here would be enough change that he would have to deal with. "Let's sit on your bed until Taylor comes back."

As she stood, Ben remained where he was, but when she held out her hand, he took it and pushed to his feet. They eased down on the bed, and Ben curled against her while she slung her arm around him. She'd done it many times in the past, but her sister had always been here. Now she was all Ben had.

She thought of his father. What kind of man gave up his parental rights and walked away from his child? He hadn't seen Ben since that day. A couple of years ago, her nephew had stopped asking about his father.

When Taylor returned to the bedroom, he gave Sierra a slight nod and sat next to Ben on the other side. "My dad needs my help at his house," he told them. "I'd promised I would help him with a project, and I don't go back on a promise I make to someone. Would you both like to come with me? It will take a few days at least, so I'll need to stop by my place and get my dog."

The mention of his pet perked up Ben.

"What kind of dog do you have?" Sierra hoped that would make Ben agree to go. Taylor didn't know it, but the one present Ben wanted for Christmas was a dog. Kat had planned to go to an animal shelter to pick one out this week.

"A black Lab named Oscar after my grand-dad. He loves my dad's house because he has a big fenced backyard. You okay with that, Ben?"

Her nephew nodded.

"Good. I saw a duffel bag in your closet. I can help you pack some clothes and toys for the next few days while your aunt gets what she needs. Okay?"

Ben released his grip on Sierra and gave Taylor a nod. Her nephew swiped his hand across his cheeks and stood.

"I'll be right back, Ben." Sierra hurried to her room and quickly packed a small suitcase.

This upcoming weekend, they were going to bake cookies for a church party for the kids. Ben loved doing it and attending it every year. Now even that wasn't going to be the same. *Am I doing the right thing, Lord? Is this what's best for Ben?*

She heaved the bag off the bed and rolled it down the hall to Ben's room. When she appeared at the entrance, he was gathering his drawing materials. *A good sign.*

Taylor closed the space between him and her. "You're ready?"

"Yes. How did you know that Ben loves dogs?"

"Half the pictures on his corkboard are of dogs. Besides, I was his age once, and I loved my dog."

"My sister wanted to get him one at Christmas," she whispered. "I'm still going to."

"I think that would be great. When I'm down, Oscar knows how to cheer me up."

She peered around Taylor to see what Ben was doing. He stuffed his art supplies into his duffel bag, then went to his toy drawer. "Is your dad really okay with us coming?" She kept her voice low.

Taylor bent toward her and said in a whisper, "Yes, most definitely."

His breath as he spoke caressed her cheek and sent a shiver down her spine. The hint of peppermint floated in the air. Trying to dismiss her reaction to Taylor's nearness, Sierra stepped around him and strolled across the room to Ben. "Are you ready?"

Ben zippered his bag and swung it off the bed.

She placed her hand on his shoulder. "Let's go. I can't wait to meet Oscar."

Struggling with his duffel bag, Ben hurried as fast as he could.

"Do you want me to carry it?" Taylor asked in the hallway.

Her nephew shook his head. When he descended the stairs, he dragged the bag down each step while Taylor and she followed. When he reached the first floor, Ben straightened his shoulders and watched them make their way toward him.

Taylor knelt in front of him. "You're strong. Good job. We're going in my car to get Oscar and then drive to my dad's. Outside there are a few people who want to talk to us. I'll take care of them while your aunt and you keep going to my SUV. Okay?"

Ben nodded, then hefted his bag and slung it over his shoulder.

Taylor opened the front door and exited first. Sierra went next, then locked up after Ben stepped outside. Without a word, she headed toward the SUV, keeping an eye on the four media teams who had surged forward. Taylor stopped them from going any farther than the public sidewalk. After he informed the reporters it would be a waste of their time to hang around the house, he told them there would be a press conference at San Antonio's main police department at five that day. The chief of police would answer all the questions he could at that time.

Ben put his bag in the car and hopped into the back while Sierra slid into the front passenger seat and glanced in the direction of Taylor. He strode toward his car, his dark eyebrows slashing downward while his mouth firmed into a frown. Not one of the cameraman/reporter teams left their places on the sidewalk.

When Taylor backed out of the driveway, one pair ran for their van and began following them. It took him halfway to his town house before he was able to shake the tail. When he arrived at his place, he pulled into his garage and lowered the door.

"Stay in here. It won't take me long to get

Oscar. I want to be away from here before they figure out where my home is."

After Taylor disappeared inside, Sierra turned toward Ben to make sure he was all right. She couldn't tell. His head hung down, his chin resting on his upper chest. Before she could think of the right words to say, Taylor brought Oscar into the garage on a leash while also carrying a paper sack and a backpack.

When Taylor opened the back door to let Oscar jump inside, Ben finally lifted his head, his eyes big but not in fear. The black Lab saw her nephew, and his tail began to wag frantically as he approached Ben. He held out his hand for Oscar to sniff. The Lab not only smelled him but also licked him. Ben threw his arms around the dog.

"Sit," Taylor said, then shut the back door and rounded the rear.

Oscar settled right against Ben and laid his head on his lap while his tail kept wagging.

Sierra faced forward as Taylor opened his garage and started his SUV. "Where does your father live?"

"Sunflower. Not far outside San Antonio."

Sierra glanced again in the back seat. Ben still held Oscar, but his eyelids began to close. She turned forward and leaned her head against the window, staring at the terrain as they passed without really seeing it.

Twenty minutes later, Taylor pulled into a driveway of a two-story white house with a front porch. Sierra sat up as an older man, about sixty-five, with short salt-and-pepper hair came outside and headed for the car. Sierra exited the car and opened the back door for Ben to climb out with Oscar by his side.

"Dad, this is Sierra Walker and her nephew, Ben."

His dad reached out and shook Sierra's hand. "I'm Robert. I'm glad y'all are here. Come on in."

"Thanks," she said with a smile. How would she ever repay Taylor and his father for what they were doing for her and Ben? *Thank You, Lord, for the help.*

After talking to his office the next morning, Taylor sat at the kitchen table and looked out the big window as Oscar romped around the large backyard as if he were a puppy, not four years old. Living in a town house with a ten-by-ten-foot grassy patch off his small patio wasn't a good match for a dog that loved to explore and run. When he'd rescued Oscar, he hadn't given a thought to the size of his yard. It had been especially hard on Oscar because he'd been working extra long hours since the multiple-kidnappings case in the summer.

The sound of footsteps approaching drew his attention toward the entrance off the hallway. Sierra, dressed in a pair of black slacks, a long-sleeve, silky gray blouse and black heels, entered the room.

"Going somewhere?" Taylor asked as he took a sip of his coffee.

She headed for the pot on the counter. "I got a call from the clinic's lawyer this morning. He wants to meet with me immediately about what happened yesterday."

"Why?"

"He's concerned one of the employees' families will sue the business." She filled a mug, then strolled to the table and sat across from him.

"Has anyone indicated they would?"

"Not that I know. I personally can't see that happening. Everyone has worked for the clinic for at least three years. We were like a big family."

"What happens to the clinic now?"

"My sister and Dr. Porter had formed a partnership. Dr. Porter's wife, Sue, will be at the meeting, too. It will be Sue's and my decision what happens to the clinic. If not for anything else, I have to go for her. She often helped out at the clinic if we were shorthanded either at the reception desk or as a nurse. I was hoping I could borrow a car since we left mine at the house."

"Dad went to the store but should be back soon. I'm sure he'll drive you to the lawyer's office."

"I don't want to disrupt his life any more than we already are. Maybe he could take me to my house, and I can get my car. Surely the press isn't hanging around since we aren't there." Sierra brought the mug to her mouth.

"When is the meeting?"

"Nine thirty."

Texas Ranger Dallas Sanders would be working with him on the case and would be here at nine. It was important that he coordinate with Dallas, so he needed to be here. "Dad won't mind taking you to the meeting. I'd avoid your house. This story has gone national. Is Ben up yet?"

"No, but I looked in and checked on him. Sleeping might be the best thing for him. He didn't go to sleep last night until late. Did you call John Yates about him being here at your father's?"

"Yes. Instead of coming before his morning

appointments, he'll come at lunch. He has more time to make the drive and see Ben." He heard the garage door going up and stood. "Dad's home. I'll help him bring in the sacks, then you two can leave. I don't want you to be late in rush-hour traffic." And he wanted to talk to his father about keeping an eye on Sierra. She wasn't a witness, but she was connected to the clinic and he still had no idea why the killer had targeted the clinic.

Out in the garage, his dad opened the passenger's door on his Jeep and grabbed a couple of sacks.

"I need to talk to you." Taylor took the bags from his father's arms. "Sierra needs to go to the clinic's lawyer's office. She has an appointment at nine thirty. Will you drive her? I don't want her to go alone."

"You think she's in danger?" His father picked up the rest of the food.

"Probably not. But I think this meeting will be hard on her. I don't want her driving by herself. She's been through a lot in the past twenty-four hours."

"I'll do anything to help her and Ben."

"I appreciate it, Dad." Taylor carried the sacks into an empty kitchen and put them on the counter. As his father set his bags next to Taylor's, he said, "I'll take care of putting this up."

Sierra returned with her purse. "Ben's still sleeping. Robert, are you sure you have the time to take me to San Antonio?"

Taylor's dad laughed. "Of course. This gives me a chance to take the morning off. My son will have to put away what I bought and fix lunch. Plus, on the way back here, we can pick up a live Christmas tree to put up tonight. Give Ben something to look forward to. I'll be right back, and then we can go."

"Like Ben, it took me a while to go to sleep last night." Sierra poured coffee into her mug. "I don't know about y'all, but you saw my house. We go all out for Christmas the weekend after Thanksgiving."

Taylor laughed. "I thought I'd been transported to the North Pole."

She set her mug on the countertop and began emptying one of the sacks. "Kat always went overboard even before Ben was born. I hope that it'll distract him some. Maybe even get him to talk. He has all these intense emotions bottled up inside of him. He needs to let them go and deal with them. I'm afraid of what will happen if he doesn't."

Taylor remembered John telling him that

when TJ died. It took him a year before he did. He didn't want Ben to go through that. He'd felt as though he'd been living in limbo—going nowhere. "I went through a situation that left me devastated and changed my life drastically. Years later, it still can affect me profoundly. John helped me, especially when he suggested I get a dog. Oscar was the best thing I did. That's one of the reasons I wanted to bring Oscar here."

"I'm not sure Ben would have gone to sleep if Oscar hadn't slept on his bed beside him."

Taylor snapped his fingers. "Thanks for reminding me. I let Oscar out in the yard. I want him to be upstairs when Ben wakes up." He walked to the back door and called Oscar. His dog bounded toward Taylor, his tail wagging when Taylor squatted down to pet him. "Guard Ben upstairs," he told the dog.

As his black Lab raced out of the kitchen, Sierra's forehead crinkled. "Guard?"

"Over the years, I've trained Oscar to follow certain commands. I've even used him in searches. When I say 'guard Ben,' my dog knows he's to stick by him unless I tell him otherwise."

"Thanks. When this is all over with, I'm going to get Ben a dog."

Her smile that accompanied her words appealed to Taylor. This wasn't easy for her. In one day, her life had changed drastically, like what happened to him when TJ died. Suddenly she'd become the legal guardian to her nephew, and from the looks of the situation, she would have to search for a new job. Maybe he'd be able to help her as John did for him because he knew firsthand how overwhelmed she would feel. There would come a time when she would realize the oppressing weight of all the changes she would have to deal with.

His dad came back into the kitchen. "I'm ready to leave now."

"Let me grab my jacket and check on Ben one last time." Sierra hurried from the room.

"I could have told her that Ben is still sleeping, but I figure she needs to see for herself," Robert said.

"Thanks for doing this, Dad."

"I'm glad you asked me. She shouldn't go alone."

Taylor's cell phone sounded. "This is Dallas. He must be here a little early. I asked him not to ring the doorbell in case Ben is still asleep." As he left the room, he nearly ran down Sierra. He steadied her. "Okay?"

"Yes and no. Yes, about the meeting. No, about Ben. I hate leaving him, but there are some things I need to do that I don't want him involved with."

An image of TJ popped into his mind, momentarily throwing Taylor off guard. Then he reminded himself that Ben wasn't TJ. "I'll take care of him." He skirted around her and continued toward the front door.

When he let Dallas Sanders into the house, the fellow Texas Ranger put a carton of files on the floor, then glanced back at Taylor. Sierra had disappeared into the kitchen.

"Come into the living room," Taylor said. "Ben's still sleeping. How's the plan for your wedding coming along?" He was thrilled that Dallas would be marrying Sheriff Rachel Young.

"I'm leaving it to Rachel and Michelle. My daughter loves helping Rachel with the plans. Michelle's practicing with Katie about walking with her down the aisle. I won't be surprised if my daughter has to carry Katie."

"They'll look adorable whether Katie walks or is carried." His fellow Texas Ranger had gone through a lot with the kidnapping case, but out of that bad situation, he'd met a woman he'd fallen in love with and would soon add her one-year-old daughter to his family. For a few seconds, Taylor thought of the family he'd once had. He didn't want to go through that kind of pain ever again.

He waved toward a chair in the living room, wanting to find out where the clinic's male nurse was. "Have a seat. Has Colin Brewer been found?"

Dallas sat across from Taylor, who settled on the couch. "Not yet. He isn't at his apartment, and no one has seen him in the past twenty-four hours. We have a BOLO out on him. His photo and the license plate number and description of his car have been given to every law enforcement agency in the state."

"Do you think he's the one behind the murders?"

Dallas shrugged. "Whoever was the shooter, he had a key to the clinic. In fact, he could have been inside the building when the employees started showing up for work."

"He would have had the code to the alarm system, which makes Colin Brewer our top suspect at the moment. Sierra told me yesterday the only ones who had the alarm code were the four with the key to the building. Besides her and Brewer, the other two are dead."

"If that's the case, that means he waited patiently until he thought everyone was there, then moved through the clinic, killing the employees.

This was planned, not a random act of violence, which is another reason to look at Brewer." Dallas half rose and stretched to place a large manila folder on the table. "The major wants you to stay here and protect Ben while working on the files from the clinic and Brewer's background as well as the other ex-employees. The box I set down in the entry hall is filled with financial and personnel information for the clinic. We're going through the court to get permission to investigate the patient files. When we get the court order, I'll let you know. You'll be notified of any change in the case. We're hoping Ben can help."

"Maybe Sierra Walker, too. She ran the office and has access to the patient files. She might even know information that isn't in the files." Taylor didn't like the fact that Sierra had to go see the lawyer when he didn't know who was behind the shootings nor the reason why. Not knowing the answers to the whom and the why left Sierra very vulnerable.

An hour later, Sierra left the lawyer's office with Robert by her side. Emotionally drained, she welcomed the warmth of the sun after sitting in an office that felt like the interior of a refrigerator.

"How did the meeting go?" Robert asked as he clicked his remote lock on his Jeep Cherokee.

"The family of Gayle Lunden is going to sue the partnership for inadequate security for the clinic. Gayle was one of the nurses."

"From what my son told me, there were security cameras that were disabled. There's also an alarm system. Sometimes you can have protection in place and still have something go wrong. Wasn't the clinic opening for the patients?"

"After all the employees without a key arrive, the door is locked until a little before the clinic opens. The alarm is off, but a person would still need a key to get inside. I often worked with Gayle. She was the nicest person. Always cheerful even when she was having a bad day. This surprises me. It wouldn't be something Gayle would do."

Robert opened the passenger door for Sierra. "A sudden death, especially under the circumstances it took place, often will leave a family stunned, grieving and wanting someone to pay for the pain they're feeling."

"I know what they're going through. I will miss my sister every day of my life. For many years—" Her throat clogged, and she swallowed several times before she was able to speak. "For many years she was a mother to me." Sierra slid into the front seat.

Robert started to shut the door, stopped and leaned forward. "Are you okay with us picking up a Christmas tree?"

Maybe decorating for Christmas would take her mind off Kat and the clinic. It might help Ben, too. "On one condition. Let's swing by my house and get some of the decorations we have up on our tree." She remembered the directive from Taylor that morning, the instruction to avoid her house. But she could be in and out in ten minutes with the decorations. "Having some of his ornaments on the tree will help Ben focus on the good times we had over the holidays and make him feel at home."

"A merging of families. I like that. We can stop at your place, so long as no reporters are out front. Where do you live?"

Sierra gave Robert the directions to the house and sat back, shoving the previous meeting with the lawyer into the back of her mind. There wasn't anything she could do about the lawsuit but let the attorney take care of it.

On the way to her house, Robert stopped at a nursery. "This is a good place to get a tree. I've gotten one here several times."

Sierra joined Robert, and for the next half an

hour, she managed to concentrate on helping him pick the "perfect" tree. "We have a fake tree. Wouldn't that be easier?"

Robert chuckled. "That's not the fun of it. Studying each tree and deciding is. Which one would you like?" He pointed at one that was seven feet and slender while the other was maybe six feet but bushier.

"The smaller tree. It'll fit your home better."

"Then that'll be it."

Within ten minutes, the tree was paid for and loaded on top of the Jeep. Sierra settled in the front passenger seat. "Thanks for the diversion. I have to confess all I'd been thinking about was yesterday. Losing my sister. The killings don't make sense."

"That's what my son will find out. Then maybe some of your questions will be answered."

"I hope." When Robert turned onto her street, she said, "Let's park in the next-door neighbor's driveway. They work during the day and wouldn't mind. This way, in case someone from the media drives by, they won't know we're here."

"Good idea. We don't want to attract their attention." Robert parked next door. "An in-and-out strike. Let's go."

They hopped out, and as they crossed the

yard, Sierra took out the key. When she reached the porch, she hurried and unlocked the door, so they would be inside in under a minute. She felt as though she'd gone on a secret mission.

As she entered the home she'd shared with Kat, turbulent emotions bombarded her from all sides. Happy thoughts immediately were replaced with the scene at the clinic. She paused in the foyer, trying to push the grief away. Not now. She had to be strong for Ben. Get the Christmas ornaments and leave.

"Are you okay, Sierra?"

"It's hard to believe that Kat's gone."

Robert clasped her shoulder. "I know. That's how I felt when my wife died. It's been ten years, and I still feel that way at times."

"When I was overwhelmed with life, Kat used to tell me to take it one minute at a time. She was practical and lived in the moment. The past was behind her and the future was always an unknown. All she would deal with was the now, and I came to appreciate that way. But at this moment I don't want to be in the present."

"Let's get what we came for and leave. Time does help."

"If this is how I feel, I can imagine how grief-stricken Ben is." Sierra crossed the foyer to the living room.

But she didn't enter. Too stunned to move, she came to a halt at the sight before her.

After going through the papers in the manila folder with Dallas, Taylor stood up and stretched, needing to move around after sitting for so long.

"I need to leave soon," Dallas said as he rose.

"Let me go upstairs and see if Ben is up yet. I'd like him to meet you, since you'll be in and out of here during the investigation." This was Taylor's fourth trip up the stairs in the past hour. After Dallas left, he thought he might come up to the boy's bedroom and sit in a chair while going through some of the papers until Ben woke up. He didn't want him to be scared, especially since it was the first time he'd slept overnight at this house.

He peered into the room. Oscar, stretched out beside Ben, lifted his head, but the young child didn't move. Taylor covered the distance to the bed to make sure the boy was still asleep. He also checked to see how hot Ben's forehead was since that was the reason he'd been with his mother at the clinic yesterday. He was warm but not alarmingly. The sight of Ben's long dark eyelashes brushing the tops of his cheeks, a peaceful look on his face, touched a place in Taylor's heart that he'd kept locked after TJ died.

He pivoted and headed out into the hall, tamping down his past sorrow. Downstairs, he entered the living room and told Dallas, "He's asleep. He still feels like he has a low-grade fever. Yesterday was emotionally exhausting for all of us but especially Ben."

"I'll meet him the next time." Dallas rose, walked to the front door and turned to shake Taylor's hand. "I'm going back to the clinic. I don't want one piece of evidence overlooked." He started to leave when his cell phone rang.

While his fellow Texas Ranger answered the call, Taylor moved the carton of files into the dining room, then returned to the entry hall. The look on Dallas's face made him pause. "What's happened?"

Dallas blew out a long breath. "Colin Brewer's car was found in a mall's parking lot."

"Good. Maybe he's inside, and we'll find him because he has some explaining to do."

Dallas shook his head. "No. He was found in the trunk, shot with the same type of gun as the victims at the clinic. Ballistics will tell us if it's the same weapon soon."

Taylor's heartbeat raced. *Is the killer taking care of everyone associated with the clinic? Is Sierra next?*

FOUR

Frozen, Sierra stared at the Christmas tree that had been knocked down, a lifetime of ornaments smashed all over the carpet as though someone went around stomping on the ones that didn't break in the crash.

"I'm letting my son know."

She heard Robert's words, but it took a moment for the concern and urgency in his voice to penetrate her dazed mind. She watched numbly as he called Taylor. As he listened to his son, the creases on his forehead deepened, and he looked at Sierra.

"I understand. I will." When Robert ended the call, he bridged the distance between them. "Police should be here soon. We need to get out."

"Why?" *Especially why did he come after me? I can't think of anyone I've angered.* "What if the guy is outside waiting for us to leave?"

"Or he's in here."

Sierra shook her head. "We would know by now. Besides, he's made his statement." She swept her arm around the room. "He's very angry. Look. Anything having to do with Christmas has been destroyed. He left everything else alone." She walked through the dining room into the kitchen and gestured at the damage in there. "See. No holiday decorations have been left intact in here either." Tears pooled in her eyes. "Every year, even before Ben was born, my sister and I went out and looked for the perfect Christmas cookie jar." She stared at the empty chestnut hutch where the jars had been displayed. "He shattered every one beyond repair."

The doorbell sounded. She stiffened.

"I'll answer it. It should be the police." Robert went back into the living room and looked through the slats of the blinds over the front window. "It's two uniformed officers," he said to Sierra as she joined him.

Taylor's dad opened the door to the police. As they entered, he told them what happened.

"Have you checked the whole house?" one of the cops asked.

Robert shook his head.

"You two stay in the living room." The other

officer drew his weapon. "Lieutenant Cartwright is on his way."

Sierra took a seat on the couch, glad the lieutenant was coming. If this had to do with what happened at the clinic yesterday—and she believed it did—it might help him solve the killings faster. The rage behind this act might indicate the murderer was losing control, which could lead to a mistake. She prayed it did. Soon.

Robert sat near her. "You okay?"

"No. In one day my life has been turned upside down, and I can't figure out why. I don't even know what I should do to piece it back together."

"Taylor will find this guy. My son doesn't walk away from a puzzle until he's figured it out."

"I hope that Colin Brewer is all right. He wasn't there yesterday either."

Robert looked away.

"Do you know something about Colin?"

His gaze fixed on the downed tree, he drew in a deep breath. "Yes. He was just found in the trunk of his car in a shopping center. Dead."

"The killer hunted him down?"

"It looks like the same type of gun was used, but that hasn't been confirmed yet. Taylor will know as soon as the ballistics test comes back."

The door chimes reverberated through the house again. Sierra started to stand.

Robert waved her down. "I'll get it." Before letting the person inside, he checked to see who it was.

Lieutenant Cartwright called out his name and flashed his badge. "You must be Taylor's father," he said when Robert let him in.

Robert nodded. "Are you working with him on the case?"

"Yes. Where are the two police officers?"

"Clearing the house."

"I'll let them know I'm here. Then I'd like to talk to you and Ms. Walker."

Sierra laid her head against the back cushion and closed her eyes. It was hard looking at all the destruction around her. She wished she could transport herself to somewhere far away. When she woke up yesterday, she had been looking forward to Christmas, to seeing Ben's face when he discovered he got a puppy. She was supposed to take him this weekend to buy his mother a present and help him wrap it up. Now all she could do was cling to the Lord and try to deal with their loss.

Memories besieged her, and she was transported back to when she was twelve years old. When her mother died, her whole life changed, and she hadn't handled it well. She nearly self-destructed until Kat and the Lord rescued her. Kat was gone, but God wasn't.

Please, Lord, help Ben. He's hurting. I'm hurting. We don't understand why it happened.

"Thanks for coming early, John." Taylor stepped to the side to allow the child psychologist into the house. "Dallas is here if you need him. But I wanted you here so that Ben doesn't wake up without seeing a familiar face."

"How long has he been sleeping?"

"Ten hours. He went to bed late last night. When he finally fell asleep, he was exhausted and fighting it all the way. Honestly, he might not get up anytime soon. He still has a fever. I've been sitting in his room."

"Good idea. I'll go upstairs and take your place. What do you want me to tell him as to why you and his aunt aren't here?"

"That I'm with Sierra, and we'll be home soon. Tell him there's a surprise for him."

One of John's eyebrows arched. "What?"

"A Christmas tree. Dad and Sierra picked one up on the way back from the lawyer's. We'll return as soon as possible."

As Taylor drove to Sierra's house, he tried to sort out his thoughts. This crime scene was no doubt connected to the killings and needed his undivided attention, but also Sierra would need someone to lean on. She'd lost her sister, but now it was obvious she was a target and possibly Ben, too. That was a lot to take in for anyone.

Pushing the speed limit, Taylor arrived at her home in twenty-five minutes, relieved to see Nash's car in her driveway. He parked next to the lieutenant's vehicle and hurried to the porch.

His dad opened the door. "I'm glad you're here. Who's with Ben?"

"Dallas and John. He was coming over anyway, so he came early. I see you got the Christmas tree."

"Yes. We came by here to get some of the ornaments from their tree, so Ben would feel more connected to the one we put up."

"I'll bring Sierra home as soon as I can. I'd like you to take the tree home and put it up in the living room. It might help Ben take his mind off why his aunt and I aren't there." He didn't have to tell his father not to tell Ben about what happened at his house. The child already had a lot to process since the shooting yesterday.

He and his father went into the living room, and Robert told Sierra he was leaving. She didn't say anything but continued to stare at all the destroyed ornaments on the floor. His dad had told him how bad it was, but Taylor hadn't imagined it to be this bad. Some decorations were ground into the carpet with thousands of pieces everywhere.

Slowly Sierra swung her head around and looked at him as though she wasn't really seeing him. He covered the distance to her and sat beside her on the couch. "This can be replaced."

She shook her head. "No, a lot of them can't. There are ornaments that Ben made each year since he was two. I don't even see any recognizable pieces of them."

Taylor took her hand, and her gaze fixed on him. "But you have Ben, and he can make new ones to replace those."

The sound of footsteps in the foyer alerted him to Nash's arrival at the living room entrance. "Ms. Walker, I need you to walk through the place and see if anything has been taken. We need to rule out a robbery. Someone could have read about the shooting, figured out where you lived and saw no one was home."

Sierra's eyes grew round. "You don't think it was the shooter?"

"Actually, I do, but I need to rule out all possibilities I can. The back door was tampered with. We have a few latent prints we took, and we'll rule out the family and see what's left. I need to take yours, and we have your sister's."

"How about Ben's?"

"Not needed. His prints would be so much smaller than the ones we recovered."

Sierra rose. "Sure, anything to help find the killer."

As Taylor followed her and Nash from the living room, he hoped the perpetrator was in the law enforcement database. If not, the prints wouldn't help to find him. And Taylor had more than a gut feeling that this killer wasn't through yet.

After Sierra went through the house, Taylor walked Nash to the door, and she went over to the downed tree. Nothing else had been taken in the house, which totally ruled out a robbery. Earlier when she opened one of Kat's desk drawers in her bedroom, Sierra had discovered what her sister had planned to surprise her and Ben with—tickets to Disney World over spring break. Kat had talked about taking her son for the past two years, but something had always come up. Now it was too late.

Sierra's gaze fell onto a red-and-gold fragment near her left foot. She knelt and picked up a part of a familiar ball. She'd glued on red sequins in a heart shape, then put gold ones over the rest of the sphere. She'd made it when she was seven with Kat's help, and then they had given it to their mother for Christmas. It had become her mom's favorite holiday decoration.

Where were the other pieces? Suddenly she needed to find them all. Maybe then she could glue it back together. As she delved into the chaotic mess, gathering what she could find of the ornament, Taylor returned to the living room.

"Sierra, we need to leave."

She ignored his words and moved to another pile of trashed decorations, suddenly determined in her mission. A glimpse of a red sequined piece sticking out of the bottom of the mound drew her attention. She reached for the fragment. A sharp edge pierced the pad of her forefinger. She jerked her hand back, a bead of blood on her skin.

Taylor stooped next to her and held out a clean handkerchief. "Ben will be wondering where we are. I don't think we should be gone too long."

She took the cloth and stemmed the flow of blood. "Then help me find the rest of these pieces. I want to glue them back. I *need* something…" She opened and closed her mouth, no more words coming to mind.

"What do you need?"

His emphatic expression, sorrow deep in his eyes, riveted her to him. He understood.

"I didn't get to say my goodbyes. I'll never see her again and…" Once more, her throat closed around the words she wanted to say.

"And you miss her."

Her ache swelled to encompass all of her. She nodded. Finally, the tears she'd held inside flooded her eyes and ran down her cheeks. "I didn't say more than a few words to her yesterday morning. We were both in such a hurry to leave the house."

Taylor took the fragments of the decoration from her palm and put them on the table behind Sierra, then sat next to her, sliding his arm around her and gently tugging her against him. "I know what you're going through. I lost my wife in childbirth. I left the house in the morning, excited we only had another few weeks before our son would be born. I came home to find she'd fallen down the stairs. I had no idea how long she'd been unconscious. Her water had broken. She never regained consciousness. They had to deliver the child through a C-section. I never got to say goodbye. She died in the operating room."

Sierra lifted her head to look at him through

a sheen of tears. The pain in his eyes mirrored what she was feeling. He did understand. "What happened to the baby?"

"He lived. My focus became him."

He has a son and hasn't talked about him. "Where is he?"

"He died from cancer a few years ago when he was six."

She sat up, blinking the tears from her eyes. "I'm so sorry."

"There isn't a day I don't think about him and miss him. I'd thought I'd prepared myself for his death, but I discovered you really can't. There were days the emptiness just overwhelmed me."

"How did you get through it?"

"My work and time have made it easier. The more I can help others the less I concentrate on myself and what I've lost. But it doesn't change what happened."

"But you wish it did?"

"Of course."

Sierra stared at the fragments of the ornament on the coffee table. "I need to make new memories for Ben and me."

"If you want, I'll help you look for the pieces and you can keep them somewhere you can look at them and remember when you and your sister made it. You don't have to glue it together." He tapped her temple. "The memory will be there."

Sierra wiped her tears away. "I'd like that. Then we should leave. Ben needs me."

Side by side, Sierra and Taylor searched the area for any part of the ornament and put it on the table with the rest.

Finally, Sierra pushed to her feet and scanned the destroyed decorations. "That looks like most of the pieces. Thanks for helping me."

Taylor stood, a foot from her.

She'd known him only a day, and yet he'd made her feel she wasn't alone—that he would be here for her. For a few seconds, she couldn't take her eyes off him.

One corner of his mouth lifted. "We need something to carry them in."

"I'll get a plastic bag." She tore her gaze from him and hurried into the kitchen, laying a palm against her hot cheek. What just happened? He was with her because of the case. That was all, and she needed to remember that. She quickly returned to the living room with the bag.

He took it, brushed the pieces into it, and then sealed it. "Ready to go?"

"Yes. Ben can't come back until this is cleaned up. I don't want him to see the anger behind this. That could totally shut him down."

"I agree. It would just add to the trauma from yesterday." Taylor opened the front door and locked it after they stepped outside.

"I don't want him to even know I came here today. Later he'll have questions about what happened to the Christmas decorations, but hopefully by then he'll be more capable of handling it emotionally."

"You could talk to John about how to handle it."

"That's a good suggestion."

When she sat in his SUV and he backed out of the driveway, she twisted around to look behind her. "What if the killer has been watching and following us?"

"As before, I'm being cautious."

She faced forward and sat back, swinging her focus to the right-side mirror. It wouldn't hurt to have both of them watching for any car following them. As Taylor weaved in and out of traffic, making several turns onto other streets, Sierra kept seeing a white car a few vehicles behind them do the same maneuvers.

She spied one of Ben's favorite places to eat. "Turn into Danny's Burger," she said at the last minute.

Taylor made a quick right into the drive-thru restaurant. "Good suggestion. In the midst of all that's been going on, I haven't eaten in hours. How about you?"

Sierra heard Taylor's words, but her attention was glued on the white four-door sedan with dark windows. She couldn't tell who was driving from her angle, but the car slowed down and pulled up to the curb in front of the building next door.

"Sierra?"

"Huh?" Maybe when they left the drive-thru, she'd be able to see the driver through the windshield.

"What do you want to eat?" Taylor pulled up to a speaker to place an order.

She peered toward him. "Eat? I'm not hungry, but Ben will like a burger with cheese, mustard and pickles."

"Okay," he said slowly, his forehead wrinkled as he shifted toward the speaker and told the young woman what he wanted.

After he paid and took the bag of food, he handed it to Sierra. "We'll be at my dad's soon."

Sierra leaned forward, searching for the white car. She didn't see it at the curb. Sighing, she relaxed, the scent of the hamburgers wafting to her. Her stomach rumbled.

Taylor chuckled. "It's a good thing I got a couple of extra hamburgers."

So focused on the white car, she hadn't heard him order. "Good. Then you won't mind me having one now," she said with a laugh and withdrew a wrapped burger.

"Go ahead. Enjoy. I'll eat mine when we get back to Dad's place."

As Taylor pulled out into the traffic, she lifted her hamburger and took a big bite. Out of the corner of her eye, she spied the white car coming out of a parking lot nearby.

Hands shaking, she turned to Taylor. "We're being followed."

FIVE

Taylor stopped at a red light and flicked a gaze toward Sierra. "A white car in back of the red van behind us?"

Her eyes grew wide. "You know about it, and you aren't trying to shake it?"

He chuckled. "It's Nash. He's another precaution in case someone was following us. He's been behind us since leaving your house."

Her cheeks reddened. "Sorry."

"About what?"

"Not believing you knew how to do your job."

As the light turned green, he threw her another quick look. "I want you to be aware of your surroundings. Two people, or in this case three, are better than one to make sure nobody is following us."

She finished her hamburger and tried to relax, but her shoulder muscles were tense, and her hands were fisted in her lap.

"I know this is hard on you, especially with this latest news about Brewer. His keys were missing. It could be how the killer got into the clinic yesterday if the front door had been locked after the others without a key arrived. Nothing was random about the shooting. The killer planned it."

"Colin was a large man who worked out a lot. How did the killer get a jump on him, especially in public at the mall?"

"The police don't think he was attacked at the mall. There weren't any defensive wounds on him—other than the bullet shot to his chest. He didn't fight with the man who shot him."

"He was surprised or knew the guy."

"Possibly or both." Taylor pulled his SUV into the garage at his dad's.

"I don't see Colin in on this. That's not him. I've known him for years."

"We'll know more possibly when we get the information from the autopsy." As Taylor exited the car, Nash drove past the house.

Sierra climbed out and watched the detective drive away. "He isn't coming inside?"

"No, he'll meet Dallas at the clinic in a while." He paused at the door into the kitchen. "Yesterday was traumatic and hectic. I wish I didn't have to ask you to do this, but I need you to go back to the clinic with me. After I checked your office, I closed the door, and no one has gone in because of the patient files. I told Nash I would deal with them once the legal papers are filed with the court. I couldn't tell if anything had been disturbed, and when you were in there with me yesterday, you were distraught. I doubt you remembered much about that time. But I need you to go back in and verify that nothing has been disturbed."

"Oh, no." Sierra put her hand over her mouth. The color washed from her cheeks.

"What's wrong?"

"I didn't think about this yesterday. When I went into my office, the door was unlocked, and you said the same to me when you first went in. I always keep it locked unless I'm in there working. Although the file cabinets are locked and a person needs a password to unlock my desktop, securing the door when no one is in the office is another precaution of the privacy of the clinic's patients."

"Who has a key to your office and the file cabinets?"

"Besides me, Mindy, the receptionist, and my sister and Dr. Porter had one. If I'm not there, Mindy goes in and gets the patients' files for the people who have an appointment. Did Mindy have her key on her? She might have opened it right before the—" she closed her eyes for a few seconds "—the shooting."

"I hate asking you to return to the clinic before the police box up the files, but I need you to. If the killer messed with or took a patient file, we need to know whose. It could connect us to the killer."

"Then we'll go tomorrow. I'll do anything to help catch this guy." She turned, put her hand on the knob and looked back at him. "But Ben must not know where I'm going. I don't want him to worry."

"I agree." Taylor followed Sierra into the kitchen. "I wonder if Ben is up." He walked into the dining room and came to a stop before going into the living room. Ben sat on the couch between John and Oscar while his dad and Dallas set up the Christmas tree.

When Ben spied him and Sierra, he jumped to his feet and ran to them. He threw his arms around Taylor, then Sierra, and stayed pressed against her.

"How are you feeling?" she asked her nephew while putting her palm against his forehead. "You don't feel hot anymore. Are you okay?"

Ben nodded, then took her hand and dragged her to the couch.

After pulling out a wrapped hamburger, Taylor gave Sierra the bag. "This is for anyone hungry. How about hot chocolate?"

Ben's eyes brightened while Sierra said, "Sounds great."

"Son, before you make it, will you bring in the boxes of Christmas ornaments in the garage?"

"Sure, Dad. John, will you help me? Dad has a lot of boxes."

John stood and followed Taylor from the living room. The second he stepped into the garage, Taylor faced his friend. "What happened when I left? How was Ben?"

"He hasn't been up long. At first he sat on the bed, hugging Oscar, but he wouldn't leave. I told him you and Sierra would be back soon. I asked him a few questions about how he was feeling, but he didn't respond. He turned away and buried his head against Oscar."

"How did you get him downstairs?" Taylor grabbed a box and passed it to John, then set a second one on top of it.

"Your dad had already returned by then. When I told Ben that your dad was bringing in a Christmas tree, he got out of bed and went downstairs with Oscar beside him."

"So he never said anything?" Taylor carried two cartons toward the kitchen.

"No. He sat on the couch and patted the cushion for Oscar. I'm not sure he would have come downstairs without your dog and the mention of the Christmas tree."

"Christmas was a big deal at Ben's house, and he's bonded with Oscar."

"And you, too. Tomorrow I'm going to try something different. I think decorating the tree today will be good for him. He was watching every move your dad and Dallas were making and nodded when they asked him if it was straight."

In the kitchen, Taylor stopped. "Sierra doesn't want Ben to know anything about the destruction at their house."

"It wouldn't help. He's not ready to handle anything else. I need to leave. I still have a few patients to see this afternoon. If you need me, call anytime." John took his boxes into the living room. "I hate to leave, but I have to go. Ben, I'll be back tomorrow. I can't wait to see what you do with this beautiful tree."

After John left, Taylor returned to the kitchen and followed his mother's hot chocolate recipe. *If John can't get through to Ben, how am I sup-*

posed to, Lord? I know I haven't come to You in a few years, but I need Your help.

As he poured the hot brew into mugs, Dallas came into the room. "I need to go. I'm going to the clinic to meet with Nash."

"Yeah, he headed that way. Tomorrow, can you stay with Ben and Dad while I take Sierra to the clinic?"

Dallas nodded. "After what happened today at their house, neither Ben nor Sierra are safe. Nash has two officers collecting any video footage where Brewer's car was parked in the mall lot. Maybe we'll get a break soon. This isn't random. The killer has an agenda that may involve more deaths. We have to stop him before that."

When the hot chocolate was ready, he asked, "Do you need any help with that before I go?"

"Nope. I've got a tray." Taylor carried in the drinks with a bag of mini-marshmallows clutched in one hand. He put the hot chocolate down on the table, then accompanied Dallas to the front door. In a low voice he said, "Call me if there are any new developments."

"Will do."

When Taylor returned to the living room, he sat where John had been, with Oscar between him and Ben. After taking a small sip of his drink, he asked, "Who's going to help me put up the lights? We have to do that first."

His dad eased into a chair, swiping his hand across his forehead. "I put the tree up. I need a break."

Taylor looked at Ben. "Do you want to help me?"

The boy ducked his head for a moment, then gave a nod.

"Great. The strings of lights should be tangle free. I took extra care last year when I put them away." Taylor opened a carton and frowned.

"What's wrong?" Sierra held her mug between her hands, blowing on the hot liquid.

"Half of them are messed up." Taylor held up a tangled ball of lights.

"Are all of them like that?" Sierra took a drink.

Taylor removed three strings. "These are fine, but—" he picked up another two and laid them by the first one he withdrew "—somehow these aren't like the others." He swung his attention to his dad.

With a beet-red face, his father stared at his hot chocolate.

"What happened, Dad?"

"I loaned them to a kid down the street for a school play."

"Okay." Taylor gathered up the ball of chaos and plopped them in his father's lap. "Ben and I will hang up the other strings of lights while you work on these."

"I'll help you, Robert. I did it for our family." Sierra crossed to his dad.

The whole time this exchange was going on Ben looked from one person to the next, his expression neutral.

"Sounds fine to me. Ben, you and I have the easy job." Taylor winked at the boy.

That produced a small smile on the child's mouth.

Sierra caught the exchange and peered back and forth between Ben and Taylor. "Robert, do you have a radio? There's a station that plays Christmas music twenty-four hours."

"In the kitchen. I'll go get it, and then we'll tackle this mess." His dad set the heap of lights next to her.

"Ready, Ben? We'll take a break after we put up these strands until they get those untangled. That might be a good time to take Oscar out back."

Ben's face brightened with the mention of the black Lab. With Oscar by his side, the boy made his way to Taylor.

His dog sensed the anguish Ben was going

through, as Oscar had done for him when TJ died. Taylor knew what both Ben and Sierra were going through. He didn't want to lose his pet. But unless he came up with another way to help Ben, how could he deny the child, who was in so much pain, Oscar?

Sierra planted herself at the kitchen window that overlooked the fenced backyard as Ben and Taylor played fetch with Oscar. Her nephew had even smiled once when the black Lab returned with the ball, dropped it at his feet, then stood on his hind legs with his front paws on Ben's shoulders and licked his face.

After stirring the beef stew on the stove, Robert joined her. "Oscar is a special dog."

"That's the kind of animal I need for Ben. Where did Taylor get him?"

"From the shelter. He'd been found alongside a highway. Oscar had been abandoned and was less than a year old at the time. Skinny. Scared of people. Taylor took one look at him and immediately wanted him. When I saw the Lab for the first time, he reminded me of Taylor. Lost. Withdrawn. My son was trying to deal with the fact TJ was dying. I tricked him into going to the shelter. I told him TJ needed the dog, but it really was for him. As a kid, he'd always had a dog. He needed one again." Robert straightened his shoulders. "That was the best thing I could do for my son. Taylor wouldn't talk to me, but he did with Oscar. Probably because his dog wouldn't talk back." He smiled and winked at Sierra.

"Ben needs a dog. He was supposed to get one for Christmas. Kat didn't want to pick the dog out until right before the twenty-fifth. She wanted to surprise him on the day."

"From seeing Ben with Oscar, I'd say any time before that would be great."

"How can I with all that's going on?" Sierra noticed in the short time she'd been at the window, the landscape darkened as night approached.

"I have a friend who has a ranch not too far from here. His bull terrier had a litter eight weeks ago. Last week he had two left. We could take Ben out there and see if he likes one of them. I'm a firm believer a person needs to pick out his own dog. When Taylor almost instantly bonded with Oscar, there wasn't another dog for him."

Sierra watched Ben and Taylor with Oscar between them as they headed for the back door. "What kind of temperament do bull terriers have?"

"Sweet, a family dog. If you say so, I'll call my friend about looking at the two left."

"Let me see what Taylor says first because if Ben finds one he loves I would want to take it then."

"And you're worried about Oscar? You shouldn't be. He loves other dogs, according to my son." The back door opened, and Robert whispered, "I won't call until you tell me to," then louder he said to everyone, "It's time for us to finish putting the ornaments on the tree. There are too many blank spots on the pine."

Taylor looked at Sierra, then Ben. "I'll be in there in a minute. I need to feed Oscar."

Her nephew opened his mouth but didn't say anything.

"Do you want to help me?" Taylor asked as he retrieved the bag of food for Oscar.

Ben nodded.

"Bring his water bowl to me. I'll take care of that while you feed him. Fill it up about three-fourths." Taylor took the dish from Ben.

"Robert, I guess we need to get started on the decorations." Sierra left the kitchen and opened the box that had the number *one* written on the side while Robert delved into the second carton. "You are organized. These all look homemade to me. The ones in yours are store-bought."

"Again, that's my son. He's a very organized guy. A detail kind of guy."

"That's good for an investigator."

"Yep, but so is the overall picture. I was a Marine MP for years and both skills were important."

"Are you the reason Taylor became a police officer?" Sierra put her first decoration on the tree, a cardboard ornament with a picture of Taylor when he was young.

"I never thought about it since I was a Marine first. I wasn't surprised when he utilized his computer skills. He could take one apart and put it back in no time. This was when he was in elementary school."

"So that explains this ornament." She held up a replica of an old desktop computer made from cardboard.

Robert laughed. "When he made it, he insisted it go on the Christmas tree. It was his big hint that was what he wanted as a gift."

"Did he get one?" Sierra put it on the tree.

"I'd already gotten him a similar one."

"I hope Dad isn't telling you every story behind those decorations. We'll never get the tree finished by Christmas," Taylor said behind Sierra.

The sound of his voice startled her, and she

whirled around, facing him, Ben and Oscar. Her heartbeat galloped at the sight of Taylor with his hand on Ben's shoulder as though the Texas Ranger had been part of their family for years rather than days. "Oscar must have gobbled his food down."

"That's how Oscar eats ever since I've had him." Taylor peered down at Ben and his dog. "We're here reporting for duty. And, Ben, it's a good thing we came. They haven't put more than a handful of decorations on the tree. At the rate they're going we won't have it finished by Christmas. They need us." Taylor headed for the box Sierra stood next to.

Ben stayed still.

Taylor glanced back. "Do you want to help?"

Ben shook his head and moved to the couch. Oscar accompanied her nephew and laid his head in his lap.

Taylor put an ornament on the tree. "That's okay. Keep Oscar company for me."

Ben laid his hand on the Lab and stroked him over and over.

As the decorations began to fill the branches, Sierra left one area empty. "At home Ben never left an area without an ornament. Let's see if he moves a few later," she whispered to Taylor.

"Must be the artist in him." He was so close

that his musky scent vied with the aromas of the pine and the beef stew simmering on the stove.

She looked up into his green eyes and felt lost in them for a few seconds. When she tore her gaze away, she fumbled a painted ornament of Taylor's family in her hand. Before she could catch it, Taylor leaned toward her and grasped it.

Taylor held it up for Ben to see. "This is my sad attempt at drawing. Maybe you can give me some pointers."

Ben jumped to his feet, grabbed Taylor's hand and tugged him toward the staircase.

Sierra exchanged a puzzled look with Robert. "What's going on?"

Robert shrugged. "Maybe decorating the tree was too much for Ben. He did help with the lights."

"At home he was always in the middle of everything. All I want to do is take his mind off what happened yesterday. No one should go through what he did. He's only seven."

Sierra's eyes filled with tears. The sound of footsteps coming down the stairs forced her to turn away and swipe away the drops of sorrow now running down her face. She had to be strong for Ben when all she wanted to do was cry until there was nothing left inside her.

When Ben returned to the living room with

Taylor, the child went to the couch, sat and put his drawing pad in his lap. Oscar resettled next to Ben while her nephew began to draw on the paper.

Sierra put a few more ornaments on the tree and couldn't bear the suspense any longer. She headed for Ben. "What are you drawing?"

Her nephew immediately held the pad against his chest. He shook his head.

Sierra backed away. He'd always let her look over his shoulder when he drew. Was he finally expressing himself about yesterday through his drawing?

Taylor moved in and whispered to Sierra, "He knew exactly what he wanted. He opened his bag and pulled out his pad and colored pencils, then charged out of the bedroom. We'll have to be patient."

Sierra peered at Ben, his head bent over the pad, his hand continually moving over the paper. "Kat was so much better at being patient than me. It's something I'm going to have to learn. It's just… Well, if Ben knows anything about the killer, I want to know, so y'all can catch him as soon as possible."

"I do, too, and there's a possibility he does know something."

Her stomach sank. The thought that he did

broke her heart. She'd hoped he had retreated into his own world and would only need coaxing to return to them with no knowledge of who the killer was or the full extent of what he did at the clinic. "I think he does. He's always been curious, always wanting to know the *why* behind things. I think he saw what happened because he would want to figure out what's going on."

For the next half hour, Sierra, Taylor and Robert finished decorating. Occasionally she would glance at her nephew, engrossed in whatever he was drawing.

Taylor put the last ornament on the tree and stepped back. "There. It's done."

"We're missing one thing," Robert said and dug into his last carton to lift out a crystal star. "We need to put this on the top of the tree. We need a special person to do it, don't you think, Taylor?"

"Yeah." Taylor twisted toward Ben. "I need help with this. Ben, will you put the star up for us? I'll hold you up."

Ben looked at him and nodded, then placed his pad on the couch and turned it over so the drawing was hidden. When he took the ornament, Taylor lifted Ben up high. Her nephew smiled and put the star that reflected all the colored lights on the tree.

Taylor set him on the floor. Ben darted to the left, removed two decorations from a crowded area on the branches and hooked them on one in the empty space that Sierra left.

She chuckled. "Now it's balanced."

Ben gave one nod, then went to the couch and held up his drawing.

Sierra's throat closed. It was picture of the Christmas tree being decorated by them. He even included himself with Oscar right by his side. For half an hour, her nephew forgot the tragedy yesterday. *Will he recover, Lord? Please protect him from further harm.*

In a darkened living room, Taylor sat on the couch after checking all the means of entry to make sure the house was locked up tight. Staring at the multicolored lights twinkling on the Christmas pine, he'd forgotten how affected he was when he put up the tree at his dad's every year. After TJ died, Taylor had brought over all his ornaments and given them to his dad. He couldn't throw them away, but Taylor never wanted to put up a tree again at his house. He couldn't take the constant reminder of TJ's death every December. Yes, he saw the ornaments when he visited his father during Christmas, and that was all he could deal with.

"Taylor, are you all right?"

Sierra's concerned voice penetrated his wall of protection. He peered at her as she entered the room. "Ben is asleep?"

"Yes. He snuggled up next to Oscar and went to sleep right away. I stayed a while longer to make sure." She covered the distance to the couch and took a seat near Taylor.

"That's good. Rest will help him. I'm glad his fever is gone."

"Me, too." She sighed. "He has enough to handle right now."

Taylor covered Sierra's hand resting on the cushion between them. "And so do you. The bodies will be released soon. What are you going to do about the funeral?"

"It's been taken care of."

"When?"

"Kat did it years ago. She wanted me to take care of Ben and not have to worry about the details of a funeral. My sister was very organized and planned for anything she could. Like you, according to your dad. I'm the opposite. All I have to do is call the Byrd Funeral Home. I'll do it in the morning." She tilted her head toward him. "The past two days have been hectic with nothing routine about them."

"Your concern has been for Ben."

"And it has to remain that way. I was encouraged earlier when he drew a picture of the tree and all of us, including Oscar. What am I going to do when he no longer has Oscar to comfort him?"

He squeezed her hand gently. "I've been thinking about that today. I think we should take him to a shelter and let him pick out the right dog for him." We? Why had he said it that way?

"Now?"

"No, we don't have to right away. Oscar is loving the attention."

"Your dad mentioned a friend with possible bull terrier puppies, but they may be gone by now."

"I'll help you get the perfect dog for Ben."

And she didn't doubt that he would. "When I came in, you looked sad. Did something happen? I know you don't have to keep me informed about the case, but—"

"It's nothing about the case." He turned toward her and laid his arm along the back cushion. "It's about my son. The holidays can be tough for me, especially since some of the ornaments on the tree are ones TJ made. I gave them to Dad because I stopped putting up a tree after TJ passed. I haven't decorated one in three years. I was fine until I sat down in here and looked at it."

She cupped his face in one palm. "I'm so sorry about your son's death. No wonder you could relate to me today about the decorations that were destroyed. You know how special they can be."

"TJ had cancer and his last year was spent in and out of the hospital. His last Christmas with me, he made me a handful of ornaments while he was in the children's ward. I was relieved he was able to come home on the twenty-fourth for a week. He put them on the tree that year. The next year, I couldn't bring myself to."

"And if we hadn't been here, you wouldn't have this year."

He clasped her upper arm. "No. I needed to. I can't avoid it all my life. TJ was my whole life after my wife died."

"I could say I'm so sorry again, but I'm learning words don't take the pain away. Every time I think about not seeing Kat again, I feel numb—like nothing is going to be the same again no matter what I do."

Taylor thought back over the past nine years, and he realized that was how he'd felt, but it was different now. "I learned you can't avoid the stages of grief. By the last year of TJ's life, I had come to accept Beth was gone. Then TJ was diagnosed with an aggressive cancer. He dealt better with it than I did. With Beth, I had TJ to take care of, but when he died, I was totally alone."

"How about your dad?"

"He was always there, but life had to go on. I had a job that required a lot of my time. It helped, but I'm discovering I haven't accepted it completely yet."

"Because of Ben?"

His throat tightened, trapping the words. Instead Taylor nodded. Her nephew had similarities to TJ, but there were also differences. Ben wasn't TJ, but Taylor wanted to protect him as though he were his father.

"That doesn't surprise me since they're about the same age. Ben, as I'm sure TJ was, is a special little boy."

"Yes," he finally said in a thick voice, checking his watch. "We'd better go to bed. Tomorrow is going to be another long day. After we go to the clinic, if you want, we can go by the funeral home and make sure everything is set up for your sister."

"I need to go by Sue Porter's house, too. She

often helped out at the clinic when we were short. She and Noah don't have any children, and her family lives in Washington. I want to make sure there are people around her. She didn't say a lot at the meeting today with the lawyer."

"Okay. I'll let Dallas know he may be here a good part of the day." No way was Taylor going to leave Ben without a bodyguard.

Sierra rose first. "I wish Ben and I didn't have to be protected. We have to find the person behind this, and I'll do everything I can."

"Tomorrow you'll start with the files. If they were tampered with, then we could have a clue that could lead us to the killer." Taylor pushed to his feet. "Will you turn on the foyer light? I need to unplug the tree." After he did, he joined her to go upstairs to grab a pillow and blanket. "I'm going to bed down in the living room so I can keep watch."

"Will you get the sleep you need?"

"Yes. Also, I called the sheriff about having a deputy drive by several times at night."

Sierra passed the room Ben was in. She'd left the door cracked. When she pushed it open wider, she peeked inside, then closed it partway. "Still sound asleep. In fact, I don't think he's moved since I left."

"Good. If there's a problem, Oscar will let us know."

At her door across from Ben's, Sierra paused, their gazes locking for a long moment.

"Thanks for listening tonight." He rarely shared his feelings with anyone, especially someone he'd known only less than two days, but there was something about Sierra that made it easy to talk to her.

She smiled. "Of course, that means you'll have to listen to me."

He chuckled. "That's fair. Anytime you need someone, I'm available."

"I'll keep that in mind." She opened the door and moved into the guest bedroom.

When she left, he couldn't get Sierra out of his head. What if he couldn't protect her and Ben from the killer? What if something happened to either one—or both?

The next morning, Sierra tensed as Taylor pulled up to the clinic after visiting the funeral home concerning her sister's burial. When she exited the SUV, the yellow crime scene tape used to cordon off the area flapped in the brisk wind. Its sound grated against her nerves. She never wanted to go inside the building again, and yet she had to. If she could discover who the killer was, the threat to her and Ben would be over. Until then they lived in fear. When she'd left him this morning, she'd done her best to make her nephew feel as though everything was okay.

A SAPD officer guarding the entrance nodded at Taylor and opened the door.

He paused. "Is Lieutenant Cartwright here?"

"No, sir, but he should be here in a while."

"Thanks." Taylor entered first and turned toward Sierra, blocking her view of where the first body had been found.

As she came into the clinic, she kept her attention on the area behind the reception counter. Her heartbeat thumped against her rib cage, making her chest feel tight. Although it was chilly outside, a heat wave rippled down her body as though someone was squeezing the breath from her lungs in front of a fire.

Taylor closed the distance between them and leaned near. "All you need to do is go to your office. I'm here with you every step. I'm not leaving your side."

If this shooting was personal, she was the only one who knew the patients, ex-employees and others connected to the clinic. If one of them came here to kill everyone, she was the best person to help the police find him. "Let's get to work. I don't want to stay here any longer than I have to. Did you find out if Mindy had her keys on her? Were there any patient files at the nurses' station?"

"I'll call Nash. He was supposed to find out, but then Brewer was found dead, and he had to concentrate on that crime scene."

"And my house." The image of the destroyed tree popped into her mind. She determinedly shoved it away. She couldn't do anything about that, but she could help search for clues about who might have done it.

As Sierra stepped into her office, she stopped and surveyed the room with locked file cabinets along one wall. Patients' written files were kept there, along with files on current and past employees as well as anything connected to the running of the clinic. Her sister had insisted on hard copies as well as cyber files.

She walked to her desk, sat and switched on her computer, inputting her password. Only two other people knew what it was—her sister and Dr. Porter. She ran off a copy of the list of current and past patients, so when she went through the physical files, she would know if any of them were missing.

As she reached for the list in the printer's tray,

she slanted a glance at Taylor on his cell phone in the doorway talking to Nash.

"Thanks for the information." Taylor disconnected his call and turned toward her. "Mindy had her keys in her front pocket. Nash also found a set of keys for the clinic on your sister and Dr. Porter."

Sierra blew out a long breath. "Okay." She headed for the nearest file cabinets and unlocked them. "Did Nash say anything about any files in the clinic?"

"Yes, there were a few at the nurses' station and one on Dr. Porter's desk."

"Will you bring them here, so I can file them away and cross them off the list as I go through all the cabinets?"

"Yes. I'll be right back."

"Close the door," she said as she went through the first file cabinet. At least with it shut, she felt more insulated from what happened. She needed that to keep herself focused.

A few minutes later, Taylor returned to the office and set the files on her desk. "Here, let me help. I'll call out the names as you check to see if they are in the cabinets. It'll go faster that way."

"Sounds great." She handed him the list, then replaced the files in their proper places before picking up where she left off. "I'm all for getting out of here as fast as we can."

Working as part of a team, Sierra went through the task quickly. Taylor stood on the other side of the drawer. His presence comforted her. "I'd like to take the computer with us. If I need to access any file, I can do it from your dad's, so I don't have to come back here. If I could, I'd never visit this place again. But I guess Sue and I will have to deal with selling the building and equipment once the clinic is released as a crime scene."

"Do you think you'll have problems finding someone to buy the property?"

"Maybe, but it's a good location." She was glad she was almost finished. She had only a few drawers left.

She opened the next one and froze, her gaze fixed on a bomb ticking down.

SIX

Twenty-eight.

Twenty-seven.

As the number changed to twenty-six, Taylor grabbed her hand. "Run!"

Sierra blinked but didn't move.

Twenty-five.

Twenty-four.

"Now!" he shouted and raced for the office door, tugging Sierra along behind him. In the reception area, he shoved the main door open and yelled, "Bomb!" at Nash and the police officer talking a few feet away.

Sierra snapped out of her daze and kept pace with Taylor as he continued putting as much distance between them and the building. He glanced at Sierra, her face pale with shock.

Boom!

The explosion lifted him off the ground and thrust him forward, his connection with Sierra severed. He plowed into the parking lot, bits of the building pelting him, his head striking the pavement. His ears rang. The world swirled. Blackness swallowed him.

Sierra's eyes fluttered open. She spied Taylor a few feet from her.

Still.

Dead?

She tried to push herself up, but a sharp pain lanced down her right arm. She peered at it. A shard of glass dug into her flesh several inches, blood leaking from the wound. Again, using only her good arm, she attempted to raise herself, but everything around her spun. She immediately closed her eyes, trying to right her world. She couldn't. She collapsed onto the pavement. All she heard was a buzzing, even when a stranger stood over her, his lips moving.

The only thing she could think to do was point in the direction of Taylor and hope the stranger would help him.

Why was a bomb in the back of her file cabinet? Why did it go off right then?

She rolled her head toward Taylor and glimpsed the man stooping next to him. Nausea churned her stomach, everything rotating. Her eyelids slid closed. She couldn't look anymore.

Please, Lord, save Taylor.

Sierra was aware people were around her. Lifting her onto something soft. The sense of moving inundated her. Faint noises penetrated the buzzing in her ears. A siren?

She wanted to open her eyes, but the effort seemed too much. She surrendered to the void.

The glaring lights hurt Sierra's eyes, but at least the room didn't spin anymore, and she could hear better—a faint beeping sound. The throbbing pain in her arm had dulled, no doubt from the meds the nurse had given her. She glanced to the right and saw part of the bandage they had wrapped around her arm after removing the piece of glass and stitching her up.

The clock on the wall in front of her read twelve o'clock. She was thankful it was noon, not midnight. The nurse promised to find out how Taylor was doing, but she hadn't returned yet. Sierra nibbled her bottom lip, trying to remain calm. Her last memory had been of Taylor lying on the pavement, still, his eyes closed.

A police officer standing guard outside her room opened the door.

Sierra tensed.

The nurse entered, followed by Robert, his expression somber. Was he coming to tell her bad news about Taylor? *Please let him be alive.* Her pulse rate kicked up a notch—then another.

"Mr. Blackburn wanted to tell you about his son. Are you okay?" the ER nurse asked.

When Sierra nodded, the woman left the room. Sierra switched her attention to Robert.

He smiled. "I'm so glad to see you're all right. I told Taylor I would come back and report how you're doing. The staff isn't forthcoming since we aren't family, but at least they let me see for myself."

So Taylor was alive. The realization lifted her spirits and calmed her racing pulse. "The doctor is going to release me. I hope soon. How's Taylor?"

"He has a concussion, scrapes and cuts, but otherwise he's okay. He wants to leave as soon as possible. He hates hospitals. I'm surprised the paramedics got him in the ambulance."

Relief fluttered through her. "How are Nash and the officer at the clinic?"

"From what I understand they were about five or six feet farther away from the clinic and managed to shield themselves behind a vehicle. The paramedics treated them at the scene. Taylor called Nash. He's still there, and that's where Taylor wants to go."

Her first response was no, but she wanted

to know what exactly happened earlier. "That doesn't surprise me. How's Ben? What does he know? Is Dallas with him?"

"Yes. When I left, John was there, too. Ben doesn't know anything."

"Oh, good. I don't want him to know a bomb went off at the clinic. He doesn't need anything else to worry about." How many times would she have to say this in regard to Ben?

"I agree, but what are you going to say to him?"

"That we were in an accident. I'm going to keep it vague. He's been traumatized enough."

"Okay. I'll go see how much longer Taylor will be and tell him you'll be fine. He's been worrying about you."

When Robert left, Sierra closed her eyes and tried to relax. She had to appear calm when she saw Ben. He didn't need to know the danger they were in. And now she knew for certain they were in grave danger. The police guard outside her room only emphasized that to her.

An hour and a half later, Taylor climbed from his dad's Jeep to assess the damage to the clinic. Nash was talking to a member of the bomb squad. He started toward him, but the sound of a door opening behind Taylor stopped him. He turned toward Sierra exiting the back seat.

He was glad she hadn't been hurt worse, but angry that she was injured at all. "I'm not going to be long."

"I'm coming with you. I want to see the damage. I'll need to call Sue and tell her about it." She lifted one corner of her mouth. "Besides, I need to know what and how it happened."

He closed the space between them, needing to remain professional when all he really wanted to do was hold her and tell her he wouldn't stop looking for the killer until he found him. She looked toward the building, then back at him, fear darkening her brown eyes.

"Did the shooter leave the bomb?"

Taylor nodded his head once. "Nash has left a police guard on the building since the shooting and no one has come near the clinic."

"Why did the shooter do this?"

"Probably there was something in one of those files he didn't want anyone to know."

"Then why didn't he take the whole file?"

"If you knew a file wasn't there, that would call attention to it. This way we won't ever know which one he didn't want us to know about. It's destroyed as well as all of the others and your computer." And whoever opened the drawer would be killed or at very least injured—which probably meant Sierra, one of the employees not there that day. He gestured toward the clinic. "As you can see, a good part of the clinic is damaged. He made the bomb powerful enough to wipe his existence from your records. I can't say for sure that was his reason, but it is the most likely."

"Then the killer has to be a patient. Those files were for patients. The employees and contract workers were in a cabinet at the other end."

He looked down at his hand. "I wish I still had the list of names you ran off. In the mad dash to get out of there in time, I must have dropped it." All he'd been thinking about was getting Sierra to safety.

A slow smile transformed her face. "I have a copy of everything in the cloud. I can recreate that list, and we'll at least have a narrowed down list of possible suspects."

"Fantastic! It's nice to get good news. Dad has a computer at the house and a printer." He took her hand. "Let's go see what Nash can tell us. It looks like the bomb squad has finished with the site."

Nash met Taylor and Sierra halfway. "I'm glad y'all are all right."

"What did the bomb squad say?" Taylor asked.

"It looks like it was homemade but had a punch, as y'all know. The timer was triggered to start the countdown when someone opened that particular file drawer. The bomb squad collected the bomb fragments and will be able to tell us more later. What they've discovered so far doesn't sound like any bomber they know of."

"The building will have to be demolished." Sierra sighed. "In the long run that might be for the best."

"Yeah." Nash pointed at the far end of the building. "At least there might be some items still intact there. Isn't that where your sister had her office?"

Sierra's expression brightened. "Yes. Can I check the rubbish now? I'm afraid to wait. With this killer we don't know what he's going to do or if he left anything else behind."

"The bomb squad went over every inch of the clinic to make sure there wasn't a second one," Nash said.

Sierra slanted a glance at Taylor. "I'm going to see what I can find."

"I'm coming with you. Nash, give me a call if anything new develops."

"I will. And the same goes with you. Did

you get any useful information before the bomb went off?"

"The files in the drawer where the bomb was were patients with last names starting with Q and R. That might be helpful." He nodded toward Sierra. "All I can say is if she hadn't pulled the drawer out all the way, she and I wouldn't have made it out of there in one piece." Which only meant he needed to stay close to Sierra, because like Colin Brewer she was a target. For all he knew the bomber was watching them right now.

As Sierra and he strolled to the other end of the building, he surveyed his surroundings, looking for possible places from which a person could watch them. That was when he noticed a crowd gathered across the street, staring at what was going on at the clinic. His cell phone had survived the bombing and now he pulled it from his pocket and called his dad, who was with the parked Jeep.

When his father answered, Taylor said, "Take pictures of the people across the street. Try not to call attention to what you're doing."

"I'll do my best. Do you want me to call to have your car towed away? It's going to be in the shop for a while."

"Yes, and I'll need to rent something to

drive." Taylor ended the call as they reached the area where Sierra's sister's office was. Flashes of finding the woman shot on the floor and Ben hiding in a cupboard flitted through his thoughts. The memory of the fright on the little boy's face twisted his stomach again.

As Sierra stepped over rubbish, Taylor helped her. She made her way to her sister's desk, which remained relatively intact, but all the things on the top had been blown onto the floor. "Do you remember yesterday seeing a box on the desk?" She indicated the size with her hands.

"No. What was in it?"

"The day of the shootings Ben had brought with him a few ornaments he'd made for the Christmas tree in the reception area."

"Wait. I remember seeing one about that size in the cupboard with him when I found him. It was by his feet." Taylor headed for the cabinet where Ben had hidden.

Sierra followed. As he opened the door, she peered around him. "That's it." After he gave her the box, she lifted the lid. "I can't believe they are intact. At least we have a few to start our collection."

"I hope Ben will put them on our tree."

"Me, too. I want to keep him engaged. He sits, lost in his thoughts too much. John encouraged me to talk to him as much as possible. Ask questions. All Ben has done is remain silent, even when I talk about things he loves, like soccer."

"I played soccer as a kid. My son and I used to kick the ball around before he became too sick. Dad has it somewhere in the storage shed out back." The second he said that he tensed. He rarely talked about TJ. It always brought back memories he'd never share with his son again.

Sierra bent over and picked up a picture frame. The glass was shattered, but the photo remained intact. She showed him Ben with his soccer uniform. "He was on a team in the fall and said he wanted to play this spring." She pointed to another one. "This was taken last Christmas."

In the photo Ben held the handles of a black bicycle with his mom on one side and Sierra on the other and a Christmas tree behind them. TJ never had a chance to ride a bike without training wheels. Taylor had planned on getting him one until his son's health rapidly weakened. He could remember his dad helping him to ride without training wheels. He'd wanted to share that with TJ.

"Are you okay?"

"Yeah. Just thinking about TJ when he rode his bike."

Sierra's eyes softened. "Anytime you want to talk about your son, you can with me. Ben isn't my child, but I've always thought of myself as his second mom."

She put the picture frame back. "We'd better go. The longer we're gone, the more Ben will worry about us. I'll let Sue know why I didn't come by today."

Again, Taylor held her hand as they weaved their way through the debris and out of the clinic. They walked across the parking lot and into the Jeep with him in the front seat and Sierra in the back.

He looked toward his father behind the wheel. "Dad, did you get any pictures of the crowd?"

"Yep. Quite a few. Take a look." His father passed him his phone, then started the SUV and pulled away from the clinic.

Taylor twisted around and held the phone out for Sierra. "I'm going to keep an eye on the traffic. See if you recognize anyone in the pictures of the crowd. If you do, I'll call Nash. He might be able to talk to him."

Sierra studied each photo, then looked up. "I recognize a few people who work in businesses near the clinic. One at the copy shop. Two at the café. One I see when I go in there for lunch. She's a loyal customer. There could be more from places along the street, but the only businesses I've been in are the copy shop and café."

"Anyone else?"

Sierra's forehead scrunched, and she took another look at the picture she'd been staring at. "Maybe. There's something familiar about this man, but I don't know from where." She leaned forward and pointed to a guy about six feet tall with blond hair, dressed in jeans and a bomber jacket.

"He doesn't work at those places?"

"No. I frequent both of them enough that I know the staff that works there. One of the waitresses at the café is also a patient."

"Okay. I'll call Nash and see if that guy is still there." He took the cell phone from Sierra and punched in the lieutenant's number. When he answered, Taylor explained why he called and described the man, then asked Nash to check out if the guy was still there.

"Yes."

"Great. See if you can find out who he is and talk to him."

"Okay. I'll let you know what happens."

Taylor disconnected the call and stared at

the man in question in the picture, memorizing his features.

"Son, your SUV will be towed later today. I'll take you to a car rental place when your head is better. There's one not fifteen minutes from my house, but you shouldn't be driving right now."

"You won't get an argument from me. I'll have enough to do on the computer once Sierra tracks down the names on the folders we didn't get to check. Sierra?" He glanced over his shoulder and saw her reclining back with her eyes closed.

She didn't move.

"She's asleep." Taylor faced forward.

As much as he wanted to rest, he kept his focus on the cars behind them. He was thankful nothing suspicious caught his attention. He wasn't at his best with his head throbbing, his stomach rumbling.

When his father pulled into the garage, Taylor's cell phone rang. He noticed it was Nash and answered right away. "Did you ID the man?"

"No. He ran away. We couldn't catch him. What took me so long to get back to you was I interviewed everyone in the group to see if anyone knew the man. No one knew him."

"Thanks for trying. I'll work on the photos I

have with facial recognition software. I might be able to ID him if he's in a database."

"Good. I'll keep you up to date."

After his dad exited the vehicle, Sierra spoke up from the back. "Do you think the killer was in the crowd?"

Taylor twisted around to look at her. Her features and posture shouted exhaustion. She'd hoped the identity of the killer would be found at the clinic. Instead there were more questions. "It's definitely a possibility. The guy you pointed out who seemed familiar to you ran from Nash. That doesn't sound like an innocent man."

"It's possible he was a customer at the café or the copy shop. I remember people's faces but not their names all the time, even when I've only seen them a couple of times."

"Yes, but I'll investigate every lead I can, no matter how small. I never know where a clue will lead me. I've had farfetched ones help me break a case wide open."

"How's your head?"

"Probably about what your upper arm feels like." He gave her a sympathetic smile. "What are you going to tell Ben when we get inside?"

"Nothing. I don't want him to know about the bomb."

Taylor shook his head, and she asked, "What would you have me tell him?"

"The truth. I'm afraid if we don't he'll find out another way. He's bright, and even if he's not talking, he's listening to what's being said."

"Then we won't talk about it where he can overhear. Knowing about the bomb will just scare him even more. He's so fragile, he might not talk ever."

Taylor slid from the vehicle, opened the back door and held out his hand to her. "We need him to talk. To share with us. So I'll go along with what you want." He started for the door into the house. "We'll go about our day as though nothing like a near-death experience happened to us today."

"Agreed," Sierra said as she walked beside him. "My bandage is under my shirtsleeve and so are my other scrapes and cuts, so he won't see anything."

Taylor reached to open the kitchen door, but before he could, it swung wide. Ben looked from him to Sierra, then flung his arms around her and hugged her tight. She winced but covered it quickly.

"I've got a surprise for you," she said, kissing the top of Ben's head.

The young boy stared up at her, his forehead wrinkled.

Sierra glanced at Taylor, who held the box of ornaments.

Ben's gaze lit on the container, recognition brightening his eyes. The child threw his arms around Taylor, gave him a quick hug and took the box. He spun around and headed into the house.

"We might be able to keep this from him after all," Sierra whispered.

"I'll let John know, though. He should be on the lookout for any reaction from Ben. Just in case."

"You're right. The important thing is that Ben has seen us returning from our errands and we are alive. At this time, that's all he needs to deal with."

Taylor waved his arm through the open doorway. "After you. I want to see what he's going to do with his decorations, and I need to talk to Dallas. When I'm not out looking for leads, he will be for me."

Taylor followed Sierra into the living room, where Ben was carefully considering where he would put each ornament. He already had put one on the tree with three to go. Oscar stuck to

Ben's side as he surveyed the perfect places to display his works of art.

"He's very artistic," Taylor said. "Not only does he draw well, but his 3-D ornaments are beautiful and well crafted. I love the one where the boy is getting ready to kick the ball into the goal. Maybe I should go look for the soccer ball and kick it around with him." The last sentence slipped out before he realized doing that with Ben would renew memories of him and TJ doing the same thing. He needed to face his son's death and deal with it.

Sierra leaned toward Taylor. "That's a great idea, but would it be safe for him?"

"With Dad and me guarding him, he should be all right. If we can make him feel as normal as possible, that will help him recover faster. Boys like to be outside when they can."

"I'm glad you'll be out there with him. Soccer isn't one of my strong suits."

With his head still pounding, Taylor smiled. "I should be better tomorrow. If I tried to run around today and kick a ball, I'd probably miss every time."

"You're still dizzy?"

He winked. "A wee bit, but don't tell anyone."

She put her forefinger up against her lips, drawing Taylor's full attention to her mouth.

He'd dated occasionally after his wife died, but no one intrigued him like Sierra. She was not only beautiful but strong and resilient. Considering all she'd gone through in the past few days, she was holding up well, and he admired that about her.

Taylor pulled his focus away from her lips. "When he's finished, I need to talk to Dallas before he leaves."

"I'll entertain Ben. I'm going to ask him to draw a picture for me."

When Ben finished putting the decorations on the tree, Taylor slowly rose. "Now the tree is perfect. Did you feed Oscar and make sure his water bowl was full?"

Ben nodded.

As Taylor left the living room, he heard Sierra ask him to go get his drawing pad and pencils. When Taylor entered the den, where his dad and Dallas were, the sound of pounding footsteps going up the staircase echoed through the house.

His dad crossed the room. "I need to go start dinner. I'll shut the door as I leave."

The minute he did so, Dallas turned to Taylor. "Your father filled me in on what happened. He told me it was by the grace of God that you two made it out alive and in good condition."

Taylor sank into a lounge chair near Dallas because his hearing still wasn't right. "Dad isn't feeling the aches and pains I am. But I agree that I'm alive because of the grace of our Lord. If Sierra hadn't pulled the drawer out all the way, I'd never have seen the bomb in time."

"And your reflexes are quick."

"That, too."

"How was Ben with John today?"

"John asked Ben several questions about how he felt, if he had any concerns. The boy remained silent, staring at his lap. John changed tactics, asking specific questions and ones Ben could answer with a nod or shake of his head. The only thing Ben did was draw a picture of a shadowy figure looking inside the window with Oscar staring at it. Before John could say anything, Ben tore the paper up and threw it away."

Taylor leaned back in the chair, laying his head against the cushion. "Did you see it?"

Dallas nodded.

"Could you tell where Oscar and Ben were in the picture? Any particular place?"

"I think it's in the room he's sleeping in upstairs. Oscar was in front of the bed looking at the figure peeking in the window. There wasn't a lot of details of the bed except a lump as if Ben was sleeping in it, but he drew Oscar meticulously. He's a good artist, especially for a seven-year-old." Dallas stood. "I gathered up the pieces of paper from the trash, and while John continued the session, I put them together with tape."

"You still have it?"

"I'll be right back. I didn't want Ben to see what I did. I figured Sierra and you needed to see it."

"Did John see it?"

"Yes, while Ben was drawing it."

While Dallas was gone, Taylor closed his eyes, the throbbing pain in his head intensifying, partly because of the concussion but also the tension that had a locked hold on him. When he heard Dallas return to the room, he opened his eyes.

Dallas gave him the piece of paper, then eased into a chair. "What do you think?"

Taylor studied the drawing, trying to assess the setting. "It might be where Ben's staying, although Oscar would have barked if anyone was really looking into the window. Besides, his room's on the second floor with no easy access from outside. What did John think it means?"

"He thinks it's Ben's way of indicating how

scared he is. Ben thinks the guy who killed his mother will come for him."

"Maybe he's overheard Sierra and me talking about the possibility of the killer coming after both of them."

"There's something else I think that might have led to Ben drawing that picture. There's a chance Ben eavesdropped on my conversation with your father about the bombing."

Taylor blew out a frustrated breath.

"Are you going to say anything to Ben about what happened?" Dallas asked.

"Sierra and I agreed not to unless he asks if something is wrong with us. He's dealing with so much right now. We don't want to add to his fear. But if he heard about the bombing, that changes everything."

"Coupled with Ben not talking so he isn't asking questions. That's a dilemma."

"When there was bad news about TJ's illness, I tried to keep it from him. But my son knew something was wrong." Taylor pushed to his feet. "Maybe what we decided isn't right. Sierra and I might need to talk to him—a conversation I won't look forward to."

"I'm going to the clinic. I'll call you with the latest."

"I appreciate the help. I wish I could be in

two places at once." Taylor walked with his col-
league to the foyer and opened the front door.
"See you tomorrow."

Now to find Sierra.

Sierra climbed the stairs to the second floor.
Earlier, Taylor had mentioned he needed to talk
to her alone. She hadn't had any time by herself
yet, but now that she was putting Ben to bed
she would. At dinner she'd noticed Taylor had
hardly said much. Either his concussion was
really bothering him, or he was worried about
something.

When Sierra entered the room to tuck Ben
in, he was already in bed with Oscar stretched
out beside him. Her nephew's eyes were wide
open as he stared at the ceiling. She sat next to
Ben. "We need to work on your schoolwork tomorrow."

He grimaced.

Right after dinner tonight, she'd talked with
his teacher and explained what was going on.
She'd always helped Ben with school projects
and had listened to him read, but that wouldn't
work right now. Ben might not want to do his
schoolwork, but he needed normalcy back in
his life, although she didn't see that happening

anytime soon. "Your teacher said your class-mates miss you."

He dropped his head and clenched his hands together.

"Do you miss them?" He'd always loved to go to school.

He nodded.

"I love you." Sierra leaned over and kissed his forehead. When she sensed a presence behind her, she looked back at Taylor a couple of feet away. He could move so quietly.

"I had to come say good night. I understand you love soccer. I've got a ball in the shed. We can kick it around tomorrow. Okay?"

Ben grinned and nodded again.

"Sleep tight." Taylor smiled and ruffled Ben's hair.

"I'll leave your door ajar. I'm just across the hall." Sierra rose.

Taylor left with Sierra, took her hand and they went downstairs.

At the bottom of the stairs, Taylor glanced up to the second floor, then leaned close and whispered, "I think Ben has been overhearing some of the conversations about what's going on. Let's talk in the kitchen."

"I should have thought of that. Ben is a curious kid. He used to listen to my conversations with his mom."

"Don't beat yourself up about it. You have a lot to deal with right now."

"Where's your dad?"

"He went to bed earlier. He insists that I sleep in my room tonight. He's going to move downstairs at midnight to take watch. He told me he didn't want to see me until I got eight hours of sleep."

"Being a parent is a lifetime job."

"No matter how we feel about it." Taylor pushed open the door into the kitchen. "Do you want something to drink?"

"Water. If I had coffee, I'd be up with your dad."

"Me, too. No caffeine three or four hours before I go to sleep." After Taylor filled two glasses with cold water, he took a chair across from Sierra at the table and slid a drink to her.

"What do we need to talk about? I got the impression it was important."

"We might have been wrong about not saying anything to Ben concerning what happened to us today."

"Why do you feel that way?"

Taylor removed a folded piece of paper from his pocket. "I didn't want to leave this lying around. Ben drew this earlier today for John but tore it into pieces before giving it to him. Dallas took it from the garbage can and taped it together." He passed the sheet to her.

Sierra stared at it, folding her arms across her chest as a chill overtook her. "This looks like a bedroom. Is it possible the killer was looking in his window?" Her quavering words ended in a whisper.

"Short of getting a big ladder, no, especially because Oscar would have barked. I'll check the ground under the window tomorrow, but it's been dry for the past few weeks, so I don't think anything would show."

"True about Oscar. A great alarm and he's protective with Ben."

"I'm glad you're thinking about getting Ben a dog for Christmas. He's so good with Oscar. With that in mind, if the bull terriers are all gone, I can talk to Dallas about getting a dog from his soon-to-be father-in-law if you want me to. His ranch is a haven for neglected and abandoned animals."

"Yes. I'd love to get one that needs a home. And Ben would enjoy seeing a place like that."

Sierra's whole face changed. Her expression of anxiety and concern turned to one of love and excitement—despite what happened earlier—when she talked about Ben and animals. That attracted Taylor. She didn't try to hide her emotions.

"Then I'll see if we can set something up in the next day or two," he told her. "I think it would be good for Ben to get out of this house, but we won't do it if I think it'll jeopardize y'all."

"I trust you. You're the reason I'm alive today. I prayed for help. You were the answer."

Protecting people like Sierra and Ben was one of the reasons he became a law enforcement officer. He knew what it was like to have his whole life turned upside down in a blink of the eye. But he had his doubts he was an instrument of the Lord. When TJ became ill, his pleas weren't answered. "What if you pray for something that doesn't happen?"

"TJ's death?"

His throat tightened. He nodded and took a drink of water before answering. "He was six when he died. He should have had a full life. I'd have given mine for him."

"Death isn't the end of TJ. He's gone home to the Lord. So has my sister. For years I was angry at God for taking my mother away. I'd have nothing to do with the church. Kat is the one who rescued me from a destructive path I was going down in high school." Tears glistened in her eyes. "She refused to let me self-destruct. She dragged me to church with her when she caught me going out after curfew. She was trying to become a doctor, and I was making her life difficult. But she wouldn't give up. I owe her everything. I started to listen to God's words."

Taylor stared at the table. He couldn't think of anything to say. He'd stopped listening to the Lord.

Sierra reached across the table and covered his hand. "Anger drove me to disrespect authority every chance I got. Love brought me back— Kat's and God's. You'll see TJ again in Heaven."

He labored to drag several deep breaths into his lungs. He had a lot to think about, but right now he needed to focus on keeping Sierra and Ben safe. "The reason I wanted to talk to you is that I think we should have Ben ask us any questions he's been thinking about. I know he won't speak, but we can encourage him to write his questions on paper or draw the word if he can't spell it. Just because he isn't talking doesn't mean there aren't questions he has, especially with us being gone a good part of the day."

"As much as I didn't want to tell him about the bomb at the clinic, I found myself wishing he would come right out and ask us why we were gone so long. Or why Robert had to go pick us up."

"We'll have time to talk to him tomorrow. You also have to get the files from the cloud and check the list of people who were in that drawer and the other two below that one. That bomb had a big punch. It was meant to destroy the whole office. And I'm hoping the bomb squad will have more on the bomb tomorrow, especially something they could run down."

Sierra finished her water. "I need to go to bed. We have a lot to do in the morning. I also need to work with Ben on his schoolwork if I can get him to do any. Normally he loves to learn, but this is different."

Taylor stood and took both glasses to the dishwasher. "You're right. I'm going to lie down on the couch in the living room until Dad gets up. The day is catching up with me. I need to get my pillow. I'll walk with you."

Sierra joined him, and they left the kitchen. She wished she had the right to smooth the lines of weariness from his face. How was she ever going to repay Taylor for going beyond the call of duty?

As she mounted the stairs to the second floor, she felt the drill of his gaze into her back. She thought back to their conversation earlier. Maybe she was part of his life now to help him deal with the death of his son. He held on to remnants of grief as though they were his lifelines. She needed to help him through the grieving process at the same time she started her own path with Kat's death.

Sierra peeked into Ben's room, and in the faint light from the hallway, she saw him lying in bed with Oscar right beside him. The curtains over the window were drawn, which she had done each night. That, too, was the reason the picture he drew wasn't about something real—just his imagination and fear manifesting itself. She drew the door toward her, leaving an opening of about eighteen inches.

When she crossed to the other guest bedroom, Taylor followed. She swung around and looked into the beautiful dark green of his eyes. The anguish of his son's passing still lingered in them.

He cut the space between them and cradled her face. "Thanks for those words earlier. I don't usually cling to something I can't change. I do need to move on."

"It's easier to say than to do, but anytime you want to talk, I'm here to listen."

He dipped his head toward her and touched

her lips softly with his—almost like a breath against her mouth. The anticipation of his kiss deepening heightened all her senses. Until she heard a shout.

"This is for Charlie!" came from Ben's bedroom.

SEVEN

Taylor spun around and raced across the hall into Ben's room with Sierra right behind him. He flipped on the overhead light, illuminating the young boy sitting straight up on his bed, stiff. What drew Taylor's attention were the child's eyes open so wide they dominated his face. When he reached Ben, Sierra rushed around him and gathered her nephew against her.

"Ben, you're all right. You're safe."

The child began to shake so much that Sierra did, too.

Taylor quickly scanned the whole room, then made his way to the window on the other side of the bed. He pushed the curtains back and looked outside. His dad had several security motion-sensor lamps in the front and back that came on when someone was in the vicinity, but all Taylor saw was darkness below.

"Honey, what happened? A bad dream?"

At the sound of Sierra's voice, Taylor pivoted toward the pair on the bed. Sierra held Ben, who was tense, unresponsive. His eyes remained open, but there was no indication he realized they were in the room.

Suddenly Ben jerked back, his gaze widening even more. Then the boy collapsed against Sierra as though all his muscles had turned to liquid. She held him against her.

Taylor glimpsed his father in the entrance, clasping a revolver. He pointed toward the stairs, then disappeared. Taylor needed to help his dad make sure the house was secured. Taylor thought it was, but he needed to be sure.

Still wearing his weapon, he rounded the bed and bent close to Sierra's ear. "I'm checking downstairs, then I'll come back."

She nodded.

As he left, he glanced back at Sierra and Ben. Her nephew stirred, recognition in his eyes now. Sierra's eyes remained closed, her face pale. He wanted to stay to comfort both of them, but first he had to make sure no one was around. In the hallway he withdrew his gun and went from room to room upstairs before making his way to the first floor. He met his father in the kitchen.

"Nothing. I even looked out the back and front." His dad set his pistol on the counter.

"I didn't find anything either. I'm going back upstairs and see how Ben and Sierra are."

"She looked scared. So did Ben. See to them, then get some sleep. It's nearly midnight, and I'm wide awake now. I don't think I could go back to bed after that shout."

"I'm not sure I can either, but I'll try after I see them settled." Taylor started for the exit.

"Son, y'all will solve this case, and life will return to normal."

Taylor laughed, no humor in the sound. "What is that?" He left before his father replied because he didn't really want an answer.

When he returned to Ben's room, the boy sat up in the bed, holding Oscar as though the black Lab was his safety net. Taylor remembered how he felt right after TJ died. His life had seemed desolate and hopeless. Oscar was still a puppy, bought to help TJ. But his son died after Oscar was a part of the family for only two months. Taylor ended up clinging to the dog rather than his son. Seeing Ben do the same brought all those memories to the surface again. A knot of emotions stuck in his throat.

While Ben's head was buried against Oscar, Sierra glanced over her shoulder at Taylor. Color had returned to her cheeks, and a glimpse of hope glinted in her eyes. Had Ben said anything while he was gone? What did the words he'd cried out mean? Who was Charlie?

Sierra kissed the top of Ben's head and rose. "I'll only be in the hall. I'll be right back." As she came toward Taylor, he moved out of the entrance.

She didn't say anything until they were several feet away from the room. "He doesn't remember anything about what he said or did. It's like sleepwalking. He has no memory of sitting up or collapsing into my arms."

"Has he ever sleepwalked?"

"Not that I know of."

"Did you tell him what he screamed out?"

"Yes, and all he did was shake his head. Do you think it has something to do with what happened at the clinic?"

Taylor looked toward Ben's bedroom before answering, "Possibly, especially if he doesn't do this. Has he ever had nightmares before and called out?"

"No. What in the world does 'This is for Charlie' mean?"

"Does he have a friend named Charlie?"

"He's never mentioned that name to me, and

I'm with him a lot. I can call his teacher tomorrow and see if there is someone named Charlie in his class or at school that Ben knows."

Taylor nodded, a frown carved deep into his features. "What if the killer said this to your sister as he shot her?"

Sierra sucked in a deep breath and held it for a moment. "Kat never mentioned a Charlie to me in the past couple of years. She doesn't date. She was focused on her career and raising Ben."

"We need to look into all possibilities. Maybe Ben will remember later. Tomorrow after you talk to the teacher, we can list all the Charlie and Charles names in the files."

"It's a common name. That might be a long list."

"Let's start with the files we haven't checked yet."

Sierra cupped his face with one hand. "You need to sleep. I'm going to stay with Ben tonight."

"That's only a twin bed. Dad has a blow-up mattress that I could put in the room for you."

"Sounds good. Although I'm not sure how much sleep I'll get tonight."

"As a wise woman recently told me, 'You need to sleep.' That goes for you, too."

She smiled. "I'm going to try, but I'm wired

at the moment. His scream scared me so much. I thought the killer was somehow in the room with him, especially after his drawing today."

"That guy is certainly in Ben's mind. I hope he'll start talking. I think he knows something that could lead to the assailant." He ran his fingers through her hair, hooking it behind her ears.

His gesture reminded her of that brief kiss they had exchanged not far from where they were standing. Not only would she remember Ben's scream, but she wouldn't forget Taylor's kiss either.

The next morning, Taylor sat at his computer in the kitchen, running through the photos of the crowd his dad took yesterday. Taylor focused on the man who ran from Nash and the SAPD officers. In his gut he suspected the runner was the shooter, there to see the results from the bombing. Was the man checking to see if the bomb killed Sierra? If so, why? Did he need to *see* that it happened? For revenge? Or something else?

If Taylor had answers to those questions, it would help him find the killer. If it was revenge, it was against the clinic and all the people inside. That meant a disgruntled patient or former employee—probably not someone randomly off the streets.

He glanced at the wall clock. Sierra should be up soon.

He had a feeling the location of the bomb was important, but when he went down the list of patients they had gotten to before the explosion, there wasn't a Charlie or Charles on his sheet of paper she'd reprinted after he lost the first one.

The sound of footsteps alerted him that Sierra was approaching. His dad was out running a couple of errands. He glanced over his shoulder as she entered.

"Is Ben still asleep?"

Sierra nodded, then headed straight for the coffeepot and grabbed a mug from the cabinet above the counter. "When he finally went to sleep, there wasn't another peep out of him. I was going to bring Oscar down here, but I didn't want to disturb Ben. He had his arm around the dog." She made her way to the table and sat catty-cornered from Taylor. "It looks like you're hard at work."

"We have a lot to cover."

"I called Ben's teacher before coming downstairs. There's no one named Charlie or Charles in her room. And she says Ben usually plays with his buddies from his class."

"The way he said it that doesn't surprise me." Taylor sipped his coffee.

"I hope you got some rest last night."

"I did. Did you?"

She stared at her mug. "Let's say I'll be depending on caffeine to keep myself awake and functioning. Part of last night, I sat on the bed and watched Ben sleeping. I couldn't stop my thoughts racing in different directions concerning what was going on."

"Did you come to any conclusions?"

"The killer is someone in the files or connected to a patient."

"I thought that, too, but when I went down the list you recreated yesterday, I couldn't find anyone who had that name or a version of it in the remaining files we hadn't checked."

"It's possible it was in the files we already went through." She snapped her finger. "Or because we assumed he took the file, so that was all we were looking at. What if he didn't take the file, but instead he planted the bomb, so all the files would be destroyed? The bomb was meant to kill us, and where it was planted might mean nothing. It was powerful and destroyed a good part of the clinic."

"You're a natural-born detective. That explanation makes sense. I went back and ran down the list. I can say there isn't a Charles or Charlie on a file. There was only one that's a possibility labeled C. H. Watson."

"I don't recall anyone who went by those initials. It could be a family member of Charles or Charlie."

"That will require you going through each file on the cloud while I try to run down the ID of the man in the crowd yesterday. If you get a name that's a variation of Charlie, give it to me, and I'll see what I can come up with. I'll go through the ex-employees and people who have worked for you as a contract worker."

Sierra took a sip of her drink. "What if it isn't anyone who has a personal connection to the clinic?"

"I don't think this is random, especially with a bomb being left behind in the locked file cabinets. The killer would have had to get the keys from your receptionist, then put them back on her, most likely when he realized you were missing. From what Nash told me, Brewer was murdered before the shooting at the clinic, and his keys were taken from him, so he could get inside before patients arrived."

Sierra sighed. She dropped her head forward and massaged her temples. "Is this what all your cases are like?"

"Some are obvious. Others are a puzzle with a few that haven't been solved. I don't want this one to fall into that category." He clasped her shoulder and kneaded her tight muscles. "I don't give up. Even the cases that have evaded me, I still work on them. A couple of months ago, I solved one that I'd been dealing with for two and a half years. This killer will make a mistake. I think he already has."

Sierra turned her head toward him. "What mistake?"

"I think he was in that crowd yesterday. Some killers like to go back to the scene of the crime. I'm focusing on the guy who ran from Nash, but I'm going to check everyone out."

"Even the ones I recognize from the copy shop and café?"

"Everyone is a suspect until proven otherwise."

Sierra went to the coffeepot and brought it to the table. "Do you want a refill?"

"Yes. Thanks."

"Where's your dad? Sleeping since he stayed up?"

"No. He's doing a couple of errands. He'll be back soon."

"Then I'm going to make us breakfast and

save some for Robert. Ben hasn't been eating very much, but I might be able to persuade him to eat pancakes. He loves them with bacon."

"You'll have to wait until Dad returns. One of the errands was the grocery store."

"Then what computer can I use to go through the files? I used your laptop last night. We both can't work on it. I've got to do something. I'm not used to sitting around and doing nothing."

"We can move to the dining room. Dad set up his computer in there during the night." Taylor picked up his notes and laptop. "I've also asked for a copy of any video the police have, including the crowd the day of the shooting. They've gone through it, but another pair of eyes on it might pick up something—but when I do that, I'll be in my bedroom. I don't want Ben to see or hear any of it—nor you, especially inside the clinic."

"Thanks. I don't think I could." When Sierra stood and reached for her mug, her hand shook. "I'll make another pot of coffee, then get to work."

As a law enforcement officer, he always had to be aware that someone might come after him because of the job he did. He was used to it but not Sierra. His gaze captured hers. "You and Ben aren't alone."

"I know. That and Ben are what keeps me going."

While Sierra walked to the counter and opened the can of coffee, Taylor left the kitchen and set up his workplace at the dining room table.

"I'm going to start with the files in the cabinets we didn't get to check," she said as she came into the room and booted the computer.

Taylor, meanwhile, concentrated on the array of photos his dad took. In one that wasn't zoomed in close to the people in the crowd, he caught a man sitting in a car across the street, staring at the bombed clinic, a camera in his hand. A reporter? Usually they approached the crime scene to do that as well as to question the police about what happened. Something didn't feel right.

He blew up the photo and homed in on the man in the black car. The picture was grainy, but it showed some of the driver's details. "Does he look familiar, Sierra?" He turned his computer screen for her to see.

Her forehead crunched. Her eyes squinted. "Yes—possibly, but I don't know from where. That's all I've been able to say lately."

"Don't worry. I'm going to have Nash see if there are any security cameras that might have picked him up better and possibly the license plate number. I also would like to know how long that car was sitting there." Taylor took out his cell phone and started to make a call when he noticed Ben and Oscar coming into the dining room. Taylor quickly put the computer in sleep mode.

Ben saw him and hurried toward Taylor, relief on the child's face. The boy gave him a big hug, then went to Sierra and did the same.

"Did you sleep okay?" she asked.

Her nephew nodded.

"Ben, do you want to go outside with me and Oscar?" Taylor asked, laying his cell phone next to computer. As the child indicated yes, the sound of the garage door opening filled the air. "Ah, that's Dad. While we're outside, your aunt said something about making pancakes and bacon."

Ben smiled.

"Let's go." Taylor led the way into the kitchen at the same time his father came in through the garage. "Do you need any help? We can do it." He pointed to Ben, then himself.

"Sure. There are a couple more sacks in the

passenger front seat. Oscar is by the back door. I'll let him out."

As Ben headed for the garage behind Taylor, he stopped and glanced at Oscar.

Taylor laid his hand on the boy's shoulder. "We won't be long. We'll go out with Oscar in a minute. Let him get his business over with, then we'll play fetch with him."

A grin bigger than the last one transformed the child's face.

Taylor and Ben quickly carried in the rest of the bags while Sierra helped his dad put up the groceries.

"I'll call you when breakfast is ready," Sierra said as Taylor and her nephew took their coats from the hook on the wall.

Taylor grabbed a tennis ball that Oscar hadn't torn up yet and followed the child outside. The second Oscar saw them, he raced to them. Ben petted him, then held up the ball and threw it toward the back of the large fenced-in yard. While Oscar chased it, Taylor panned the area. He couldn't let down his vigilance with Ben or Sierra.

After lunch, Sierra gave Taylor the last plate to put in the dishwasher. "Did you call Nash about the man in the car?"

"Yes. He'll see what he can get, but as he crossed the street to check on the guy I wanted him to, he didn't see a black car anywhere near the area."

"So that means the person drove off between the time we left and you called him about the guy in the crowd." She leaned against the counter, clutching the ledge. "I wonder if he was taking a picture of us instead of the building."

"Or both. That's definitely possible." He walked toward the dining room, and Sierra followed.

"Did you tell John about what happened last night with Ben?"

"Yeah. He's going to see if he'll draw him a picture of it. If so, then he'll ask him questions about his drawing, ones he can answer with a yes or no or point to something on the paper." He sat in front of the computer he was using, and Sierra did the same. "He thought it was a good sign that he spoke out even though he was sleeping." He shrugged. "I have a feeling he won't remember anything. I never remember my dreams."

"Sometimes I do, but usually they will fade from my memory quickly. I tried to get him to tell me last night. I asked him several questions, but he didn't respond at all."

"John and I are going to kick the soccer ball around with Ben at the end of his session. He thinks having Ben do physical exercise will help. He's bottling up a lot of emotions and that can help him release them."

Sierra sighed. "While I'm stuck in here going through the files, which hasn't produced anything yet. Still no Charles or Charlie in them." Sierra pulled up the next patient file on her computer.

"Anything close to those names?"

"One Charlotte and two Charlenes. I've gone through the three drawers we didn't get to check. Now I'll start at the beginning and go through the ones we looked at in my office."

"Make notes on anything close, then we'll dig deeper into those files. Don't only look for Charlie but for anyone who was upset with the clinic or doctor."

For almost an hour, she delved deep into the files, jotting down Bruce Lockhart, who got angry when he didn't get the drugs he wanted, the Aikens, who were turned into Child Services because of suspected abuse of their little boy with a middle name of Charles, and a man who was diagnosed with Parkinson's disease and didn't take the news very well.

John popped his head into the room from the

kitchen. "Ben is excited about kicking the soccer ball. Are you ready?"

Taylor put his laptop to sleep and rose. "I need some exercise. I've been sitting too long." He slid his cell phone to Sierra. "Answer it if Nash calls and let me know what he found out."

She nodded and watched the trio leave. She went back to work for another thirty minutes. When she finished five more patient files and added another possible name to her list, she decided to refill her water and move around. She paused at the kitchen window that overlooked the backyard.

Ben was running with the ball with John right behind him, as though trying to steal it away from her nephew. Suddenly he came to a halt and kicked it toward Taylor. Then as John tried to take the ball away from Taylor, he tapped it back to Ben, who kicked it into a makeshift goal. Ben jumped up and down, pumping his arm in the air. When he turned, she saw the biggest grin on his face. Seeing Ben having fun brought tears to her eyes. She pivoted away from the window, swiping the wetness from her cheeks.

The sound of Taylor's cell phone drew her quickly back into the dining room. She snatched it off the table by her computer, looked at the screen and answered it. "Hello, Nash. I'm answering for Taylor. He's outside right now with Ben."

"Sierra?"

"Yes, sorry. I forgot to identify myself. Did you find out anything on the car and the person driving it?"

"I wish I had good news, but the car was stolen. We got a better photo of the driver from some of the video footage we got but haven't been able to ID him yet."

"Can you send the photo to this phone?"

"I will. I'll keep y'all informed if we find the man or the car."

"Thanks, Nash."

Sierra sat down in front of her computer and started working where she left off. After a few moments, she found herself staring at the screen at the blinking cursor. She'd looked at the guy in the car, but she hadn't been able to tell Taylor she knew him for sure. She hoped Nash had a better shot of him or Taylor could make it clearer on the one Robert took.

She hadn't said anything to Taylor, but ever since Ben had said *this is for Charlie*, something had been bothering her. Did she know something? It was as if the nugget of information was at the edge of her thoughts, and every time she reached for it, it vanished from her mind.

"The search must not be producing any results," John said from the doorway into the kitchen.

"I'm getting some names and a few cases where people weren't pleased with the service at the clinic, but nothing that should make a person kill everyone."

John moved farther into the dining room. "I've learned through my studies and from clients over the years that sometimes there's no rational reason why someone acts a certain way—at least to others. In his mind it makes sense, or it's meeting a need like revenge. Look at everything that might be a problem to someone."

Revenge. She couldn't imagine killing so many for any of the reasons she'd come up with so far.

"It can be hard to put yourself in another's mind." John took the chair Taylor sat in. "Some people flip out over what another would think wasn't a good reason."

"Are Ben and Taylor coming inside?"

"In a few minutes. I wanted to see you without Ben around."

"How did the session go today?"

"Okay. Ben did draw a picture that he didn't tear up this time."

"What was it of?"

John withdrew it from his coat pocket and unfolded it. "What do you think?"

It was a drawing of a man with a backpack. It was hard to tell how tall he was, but his build was thin. He was bald and wearing glasses. "Do you think this is the shooter?"

"I asked him where the words *this is for Charlie* came from, and this is what he drew."

"This is the shooter!" She felt a mixture of elation and fear shoot through her.

"Not necessarily. It could be from something totally unrelated."

"But you think it isn't?"

"There's a good chance it is because as he drew he frowned and his hand shook the whole time. Whoever this is had a profound effect on Ben." John stood up. "I have to go. I still have some clients who come to see me after school. Keep the drawing. I didn't get a chance to show Taylor. If he needs to call me, I'll be free after six tonight."

Sierra walked with the child psychologist to the front door and made sure it was locked after John left. The sound of Ben and Taylor coming inside hurried her to the table. She folded up the drawing and stuck it under another piece of paper.

As Ben and Taylor came into the room, Sierra asked, "Did y'all have fun?"

A smile still on his face, Ben nodded.

Taylor raked his hand through his hair. "Great exercise."

Possibly too much, she thought judging from Taylor's heavy breathing and sweaty forehead, especially after the day they had yesterday.

Robert walked into the room then. "And now it's time for your schoolwork." He approached Ben. "Let's get something to drink and head to the den."

Taylor waited for them to leave the room, then he came up close to Sierra. "What did John say?"

Sierra slid the drawing out and showed it to Taylor. "He thinks it's a picture of the shooter. Granted, it isn't a photo, but it does tell us some things about the man possibly."

"He wears glasses. He's thin and bald. That might help us. Does that fit the description of anyone you remember at the clinic?"

"Not right off. I'll have to think about it. So many people come and go."

Taylor woke up his computer and pulled up the photo of the guy in the car yesterday. "Let me see if I can enhance this any more. The guy in the car might have on glasses."

"If it's the killer, I guess I should be glad Ben saw him, but I'm not. To think he watched the killer murder his mother… No wonder he can't say anything. The thought robs me of words, too."

"I think the drawing is the killer. Look." Taylor turned the computer screen toward her to show her the guy in the car had on glasses. "I know it looks like he has dark hair, but that could be a wig."

"If that's the case, that means the killer did it because of Charlie?"

"Yes. Did Nash call?"

She nodded. "He's sending you the video he collected of the street in front of the clinic at the time we were there. He's gone through the footage and got the license plate number on the black car. It was reported stolen."

On his laptop, Taylor pulled up the emails with the security camera footage. "It looks like we both have a lot to do."

"I'm getting some more water. Do you want me to get you something to drink?"

"Yeah. Water is fine." Taylor's cell phone buzzed.

Sierra left as he answered the call. After refilling their glasses, she headed back into the dining room, only to find Taylor's shoulders hunched forward while he listened to whoever was on the other end of the call. When he disconnected, he looked at her, a pale cast to his tanned features.

"What happened?" she asked in a soft voice, almost afraid to know.

EIGHT

"There's been another shooting. This time at an insurance office. Nash thinks it's the same killer," Taylor said in a whisper, not wanting Ben to overhear.

Sierra nearly spilled the water as her hands began to shake. She sank into the nearest dining room chair at the opposite end and set the glasses down. She opened her mouth to say something but instead snapped it closed.

Taylor came to her. "Are you okay?"

"No." She looked up at him, her eyes dark and troubled. "Ben can't know what has happened. He has enough to deal with." She shook her head. "I seem to be saying that a lot."

"Sierra, so far he's the only one who might have seen the killer. No one at the insurance office survived."

"How many were killed?"

"Four."

Sierra closed her eyes and clasped her arms to her chest for a moment. When she opened her eyes, determination hardened them. "Which insurance office? I work with a lot of them."

"Ryan Morton Insurance Brokerage."

"That's one I've worked with. I've dealt a lot with them. When? How? The office is in a shopping center. No one saw anything?"

"It happened early, right after the staff arrived. The killer was probably watching. The employees came in the back way, and that was how the killer got inside. He most likely followed the last person inside before the back door was secured. Same MO as the clinic and I'm reasonably certain the same gun, although the ballistics report hasn't confirmed that yet. The front door was locked, and the blinds were pulled."

"How were they found?"

"A friend was meeting the secretary for lunch. When she didn't show up and she couldn't get her on the phone, the woman went by the office. She called the police when she couldn't get into the office nor see in. She knew the office was never locked during business hours and the blinds were always open."

"How about security cameras?"

Taylor frowned. "He avoided them, then shot them out, same as with the clinic."

"How about behind the shopping center?"

"There's one camera that shows the area behind the stores and offices. It was conveniently shut down right before dawn. The security firm came out to the shopping center about ten and replaced it. No image of who sabotaged it."

Sierra dropped her head into her hands. "Is this guy picking businesses randomly or is there a pattern?" She inhaled a deep breath, then exhaled slowly as though she were fighting to keep herself composed.

"I don't know for sure, but I still think this is personal and both the clinic and the insurance office are tied to the man. Now we need to concentrate on the patients at the clinic who were connected with Ryan Morton's insurance agency. Nash called Dallas, and he's on his way to the crime scene. He'll take pictures of it and send them to me. Right now, Ben is our best lead besides the video Nash sent me with the guy in the black stolen car."

Sierra shot to her feet. "Let's get to work. What if he's planning another shooting? He's got to be caught before more people die." As she walked to her computer, she halted and whirled around. "Ben does not need to know about this.

He can't even process his mother's death. I'm not even having her memorial service until this is settled. It would put him in too much danger on top of all the trauma he's gone through."

"I agree. I know what you're going through."

She started to turn, paused and glanced back at him. "I tremble to think of what could have happened to Ben and me if you hadn't helped us. I can't thank you enough."

"It's my—"

"Don't tell me it's your job. It's more than that."

The sound of Sierra's cell phone buzzing echoed through the room. She hurried to answer it.

Taylor retook the chair in front of his laptop. Sierra was right. His connection to this case was more than his duty. At first it was all about the case, but now there was something about Sierra that kept him at her side. Two days ago, he would have said it was Ben that drew him, but not now. His wife died nine years ago, and in all that time he'd never been interested in another woman. Until Sierra.

When she finished her call, she said, "That was Mindy's mom. She wanted me to know about her funeral arrangements. They are Sunday at four at the River Walk Funeral Home. I told her I would be there. We worked closely together. She was a really good friend."

He wanted to tell her not to attend, but he knew the importance of saying goodbye to people you were close to. "I understand. I'll take you. Dallas can stay with Dad and Ben. And I'll find out if Nash is putting any police officers at the funeral home. When are the other funerals?"

"The next one is the day after. Maria Cruz. She was one of the nurses."

"We'll see how it goes at Mindy's. The most important thing is your life."

She nodded. "I'll go along with your judgment."

"If I get there and think it's too dangerous, will you leave right away?"

"Yes. I'm all Ben has. I'll do what you say."

Taylor shoved to his feet, his muscles cramping. "I've got to make the plans for the trip. It's going to be a long day."

"Sunday? The funeral won't be long, according to Mindy's mom."

"I mean both days. Planning will take hours."

"I want to finish going through the files, so I can help you."

He smiled at her. "I appreciate the help. Nash has people working on different angles while we work this one."

As he paced, he ran through a list of tasks he needed to do before the funeral. First and foremost, he wanted as good a photo of the killer as he could come up with. He didn't want Sierra to be worried, but he knew of occasions when the killer attended his victim's funeral.

Hours later, Sierra relaxed back against the dining room chair. "I'm finished. I've gone through all the files and have my list of possibilities either because of the name *Charlie* or concerns with the clinic or an issue there that I know about."

"Good. Nash and Dallas will be here soon. I'm going to run off the photo I cleaned up of the guy watching after the bombing and the one in the black car."

"Then I need to put Ben to bed. I don't want him overhearing anything about the funeral on Sunday or strategies for catching the killer." She wasn't sure she wanted to hear it herself, but she realized a part of her wanted—actually needed—to be part of the investigation. She was doing what she could to find the murderer before he killed more innocent people.

Sierra headed for the den, where Ben was watching TV with Robert and Oscar. When she entered, her nephew lay on the couch, his eyelids halfway closed. The day was catching up with him. She sat near him and felt his forehead, in case he was having a relapse from his illness a few days ago. His skin was cool to the touch.

She shook Ben's shoulder.

He groaned.

"Don't wake him. I'll carry him up to his bedroom. For the past half hour he's been fighting sleep." Robert stood and scooped her nephew up into his arms.

Sierra followed the pair up the stairs to Ben's bedroom. The blow-up mattress she had used last night was still there, and she intended to use it tonight, too. Ben's emotions were all over the place. If he was kept entertained or active, he relaxed and even smiled a few times. But the second he started retreating into himself, his shoulders hunched and his head dipped forward, a scowl on his face.

Robert gently placed him onto the bed. "We were watching a comedy earlier, and Ben actually laughed once." He clasped her shoulder. "You're doing a great job. The best thing you can do is be here for him, which is what you're doing."

"Thanks, Robert. I needed to hear that today." She'd spent most of the time sitting in front of the computer. Tomorrow, she wanted to be out in the backyard kicking the soccer ball around with Ben. She needed the exercise.

As Robert ambled toward the hallway, Sierra pulled the coverlet up to Ben's shoulders, then leaned down and kissed his forehead. He didn't move. Oscar settled along Ben's left side and laid his head near her nephew's.

She left the night-light on and the door ajar when she exited the room and descended the staircase with Robert. "I don't know what we're going to do without Oscar."

Robert nodded. "Taylor became very attached to Oscar after TJ died. He did wonders helping bring Taylor through his grief."

"Oscar has a gift. He can sense when someone needs him. Ben will need a special dog to take Oscar's place."

"There are a lot of animals that need a home." Robert frowned. "I called my friend, but he didn't have any bull terrier puppies left."

"Taylor told me Dallas's future father-in-law has abandoned dogs at his ranch. One gave birth to some puppies who are ready to be adopted."

A knock sounded on the front door as Taylor came into the foyer. "It's Nash and Dallas. They called me a couple of minutes ago. I didn't want them to ring the doorbell with Ben going to bed."

"Well, this is my time to retire to my bedroom. I'll relieve you at two, son." Robert headed back up the stairs.

Taylor checked to see who it was outside on the porch and then let Nash and Dallas into the house. Exhaustion carved deep lines into their faces. The investigation drove the law enforcement agents involved nearly twenty-four hours a day, especially with the second shooting spree.

"Let's go into the dining room." Taylor gestured in that direction.

Sierra paused at the entrance into the kitchen. "Does anyone want coffee?"

Everyone nodded. Sierra quickly filled four mugs with the hot brew, then made another pot of coffee for later.

When she returned to the "command post," as she'd come to refer to it in her mind, she sat at the dining room table next to Taylor while Nash and Dallas took the seats across from them.

"Any additional information on the case?" Taylor asked.

"We got the ballistics report back. It was the same gun as the clinic shooting." Dallas sipped his coffee.

Nash put his mug down on a coaster. "And the car out in front of the clinic yesterday was found not a block from the shooting while another vehicle was reported stolen nearby, possibly the killer's new getaway car. There's a statewide BOLO out on it."

Taylor wrote on his pad. "Any useful forensics in the car?"

Dallas frowned. "No, and any cameras nearby didn't pick up the driver. But a picture was taken of a guy wearing a black hoodie and black pants near the more recently stolen car after the shooting."

Taylor grabbed the copies he'd run off of the man sitting in the car yesterday after the bombing. "I managed to get a pretty good photo of the man from your video footage." He handed everyone a copy.

Sierra stared at the guy who could possibly be the killer. Dark, short hair. Black glasses. Thin face. Narrow lips. "He does look familiar. Not quite like Ben drew but similar in a few ways." Where had she seen this person before? "But I don't know why. Possibly a client at the clinic. There are no pictures in the files to compare this to."

"Let put this out all over the news asking if anyone has seen this guy. He's a person of interest in the shootings. Someone may recognize him." Nash took a gulp of his drink. "It's the best lead we have at this time."

"I have made a list from my files of people who weren't happy with the clinic or someone there. Also, I have put down people who are named Charlie, Charles or any name similar to that like Charlotte. Now I need to get photos of these people and see if one matches the photo of the possible suspect."

"Sierra, I can help you with that," Taylor said. "The person treated at the clinic might not be the killer, but he might be connected to that person, especially if we consider what Ben called out and drew, which is a bald-headed man. The dark hair could really be a beanie he was wearing—or a wig. It's hard to tell for sure. 'This is for Charlie,'" he said, echoing what Ben had called out in the night. "It sounds like revenge for Charlie."

"Like a person dying? Or the killer didn't like something concerning a treatment or a diagnosis?" Dallas pushed to his feet. "Is there more coffee?"

Sierra nodded, and as Dallas went to the kitchen, she asked, "Did the killer say that to each victim or just to my sister? Maybe we should concentrate on her patients first."

Taylor turned to her. "Let's start with putting out the photo I cleaned up and see if we get any tips from the public." Then he said to Nash,

"Meanwhile, Sierra and I are going to the funeral for Mindy Carson Sunday afternoon. Are you going to have police there?"

"Yes, some in uniform, others in plain clothes. I'll make them aware you and Sierra will be there. I'll have a couple of them—ones you know, Taylor—nearby y'all."

"Good. It's been a long day. First thing tomorrow when I'm more refreshed, I'll go through Sierra's list. Ben hasn't said anything since his mother was killed except that one phrase. He didn't remember doing that when he woke up, but it might be his mind's way of getting it out." As Dallas returned from the kitchen, Taylor asked him, "I'll need you here helping track down the people on the list and also need you with Ben on Sunday when we leave for the funeral."

"I was planning on it. Right now, we're waiting on any forensics from today's shooting and the bombing yesterday. Maybe something there will help narrow down the suspect or at least help the case when he's caught."

As the three law enforcement officers planned their next moves, Sierra fought a yawn. Even with a cup of coffee she couldn't stay up much longer. She found herself starting to nod off like her nephew.

A hand grasped hers. "Go to bed, Sierra. We're about finished, and tomorrow's going to be another long day for all of us."

She slanted a look at Taylor. The kindness in his eyes quieted all her fears concerning going to Mindy's funeral. She would be in safe hands.

"You're up early. How long have you been working?" Taylor asked as he caught sight of Sierra sitting at the dining room table, staring at the computer screen.

She gasped and looked at him. "I didn't hear you come down. You need to wear a bell or something to let me know when you're nearby. In fact, I think I remember I put one on your Christmas tree. I'm sure I can find it for you."

He chuckled. "I'll pass, but I'll try to remember to make some noise as I enter a room. Any coffee left?"

"Yes. I just made it. I haven't been down here long. I'm hoping we can find the killer before Mindy's funeral tomorrow."

"What are you working on?"

"I'm looking at the patients who used Ryan Morton as an insurance broker. Then we can see who is on my other list."

"Good. You're a natural at this."

She lost herself again in the files she was looking through.

As he entered the kitchen, he couldn't forget Sierra using *we* as though she was his partner. In the past couple of days, it had become more and more true. He even found himself thinking of them as a *we*. That thought stopped him in mid-action of pouring his drink. He could see them dating when this case was over. He wanted to continue seeing her and Ben. Before he spilled the coffee, he set the carafe down on the counter. His feelings for Sierra were deeper than he thought.

And Ben was becoming special to him. He was going through something traumatic and needed a lot of support. Sierra would have her hands full—mourning her sister's death and at the same time trying to be strong for her nephew and providing a safe home for the boy.

Taylor shook the thoughts from his mind. His focus had to be the case right now. Nothing else. If anything happened to either one of them, he would blame himself for not paying enough attention.

"What's wrong, Taylor?"

Caught off guard, he stiffened and whirled around. But he saw Sierra and immediately relaxed, although his heart still pounded against his chest. "I didn't hear you come in here."

"Good. Now you know how it feels." She smiled. "Actually, I thought you got lost between the dining room and the kitchen."

"Cute. Just thinking." No way would he tell her she was the subject of his thoughts.

He finished pouring his coffee into a mug, then followed her to their command post. "I'm going to start looking for pictures to match the names on your list." As he put in the first search, he asked, "Where's Dad?"

"He's in the den. He wanted to catch the news. I told him that a photo of a possible suspect hopefully will be on it."

"Nash said it would go out last night. He'll call me later with any good leads from the picture."

"Yeah, people are just getting up and starting their day. Some won't even look at the news until this evening. And last night was too late for the photo to be shown on the late-night news."

"If it's the killer, he'll probably see it, too. He might leave San Antonio."

"That's why we have a statewide BOLO out on him. The search can be expanded, especially if I can match it to a patient. Nash has some officers going through the insurance company's records, especially when you are finished with your list of patients using Ryan Morton Insurance Brokerage."

Sierra picked up a pencil next to her computer. "Are all your cases this intense?"

"Some."

"Do you live and breathe a case?" She began to doodle on a sheet of paper.

"Yes. Each one is a challenge to me."

"Well, this one is certainly providing that."

Taylor turned his attention to the list of people he needed to find a photo of, but his eyes were continually drawn to Sierra. She was definitely a distraction. Maybe he should work in the kitchen. Yet he liked having her nearby. He didn't feel so alone.

When his dad came into the dining room a short time later, he paused between Taylor and Sierra. "I'll fix breakfast when Ben gets up. Don't worry about him. I'll make sure he does his schoolwork and gets some exercise with Oscar. Good for both of them."

"Thanks, Robert. Ben has become attached to both of you. I've been praying each day that he'll start talking. Until he does, he's keeping his fear and pain inside, and that isn't good."

"I'm glad he's here. It makes me think about how it was when Taylor was his age." Robert clapped his hand on Taylor's shoulders. "And until this case I haven't seen my son nearly enough." He started across the living room. "I think I hear Ben. I'll go check if he's up."

Not five minutes later, Ben made his way down the stairs with Oscar.

Robert poked his head into the room. "Oscar needs to go outside. We'll be in the backyard." When Taylor opened his mouth to tell him to survey the surroundings before stepping outside, his father waved his hand. "Son, I know the drill. Remember, I was in the police force for the Marines."

"Is he why you became a police officer?" Sierra asked when his father left.

"He was always my role model growing up, and sometimes I used to think he could read my mind."

"I wish Ben had a role model. His dad didn't want to be involved with him. Thankfully Ben doesn't know the whole story. Now it's up to me to make him feel he's loved and special."

"That's important for all children."

The idea that Sierra and Ben were in danger because of the killer he was looking for super focused Taylor's attention on his task—finding photos of the people Sierra was gleaming from the patient files. Hours later, he stood and stretched while staring down at the computer screen with a picture of a man who looked similar to the one whose image was being blasted all over the news. Had he found the killer?

NINE

"Have you got something?" Sierra asked, tired from staring at the laptop screen for hours. She was almost through the files and had a good list of patients who had insurance through Ryan Morton.

The corners of Taylor's mouth slowly lifted as he looked at her. "I've got a match with the photo of the guy in the car."

"Who?" She rose and came around to see the man.

"That's Max Richardson."

"He's on my list of Ryan Morton's clients. I've looked at so many files these past couple of days. Let me pull up the file associated with him. I don't think he was a patient." Sierra retook her seat and began searching the patient archives.

"But you put him on your list for the clinic. Why?"

Sierra clicked open a patient file for Charlene Richardson. "The patient was his daughter. He and his wife, Josie, came in with her. She was eight years old and suffering from a rare disease."

Taylor stood behind Sierra and read the file over her shoulder. "She died two Christmases ago. Was Charlene the reason you flagged him and put him on your list?"

"Yes, but there's something else. I don't remember it all, but my sister was her doctor. I skimmed Charlene's file yesterday but I need to read Kat's notes. It should tell me more."

"Do you want more sweet tea?"

"Yes, please." She passed the empty glass to him, her hand brushing against his. A thrill shot through her. The memory of the brief touch of their lips the other night made her wonder what it would feel like being really kissed by him.

"Be back in a sec."

Stay focused on the task, Sierra.

She watched him disappear into the kitchen and dragged her attention from the doorway. Quickly she found Charlene Richardson's file and flipped to her sister's notes. Sometimes Kat's handwriting was hard to read, but she had learned to decipher it over the years. In the middle of the task, Taylor set her glass near her and quietly went to work at his laptop. She chanced a quick peek at him, then returned her focus on what was before her. She and Ben would not live their lives scared this man would come after them.

The last notes Kat wrote in Charlene's file made goose bumps flash up her arms and throughout her body. "This is what Kat said in her last entry. 'Mr. Richardson was livid when I had to tell him and his wife the new study wouldn't accept Charlene as a subject. She didn't fit the protocol. All I can do is try to make her life as pain free as possible, but Charlene is too near death to qualify.' This note was dated two weeks before Christmas two years ago."

"When did Charlene die?"

Sierra read an addendum to Kat's notes. "Two weeks later, on Christmas. My sister never told me how dire the situation had been. She didn't like to discuss her work at home. There were notes throughout the chart that insurance wouldn't pay for an experimental drug that would delay her death and increase her quality of life. That part I remember as far as the insurance company denying my sister's requests."

"Definitely a motivation to push a father over the edge, and it connects the two shootings. But why did he wait two years?"

"It also explains why at Christmas. But why

not last year? What triggered him to kill now?" Sierra reclined back and sipped her tea, staring at the screen. "The cost of drugs has skyrocketed, and ones that are for only a few people are out of range for them."

"I'll delve into his life. For this kind of rage after two years, something had to set him off." Taylor snatched his cell phone from the table and pushed to his feet. "I'm going outside. I don't want Ben to overhear any of this. I'm calling Nash and Dallas."

As Taylor left the dining room, Sierra wondered if this meant the case would come to an end soon. Then she and Ben would be safe and could go back to their home.

And face that Kat's gone.

Working with Taylor had allowed Sierra to ignore her grief over losing her sister—her best friend and her surrogate mother.

Tomorrow was the first of the funerals for the victims. There'd be no more time to avoid thinking of what would change in her and Ben's lives. On top of that, in preparation for her and Ben returning to their home, the place had to be cleaned, all evidence of the shattered ornaments and smashed decorations removed.

But also, she needed to address the feelings she was developing for Taylor. She cared for him—no, she was falling in love with him. And after only five days. She'd always been leery of men and only dated occasionally. Now, though, she wanted to put her past behind her and hope she could move forward.

But would Taylor understand about her past?

Taylor pulled up behind Nash and three SAPD police officers and exited his rented SUV at Max Richardson's residence. Dallas had relieved him at his dad's house, so that he could be part of the apprehension of the suspect. Everything they'd discovered in Richardson's background so far pointed to his being the killer.

The car registered to Richardson was sitting in the driveway. He prayed the man was inside the house. He wanted this nightmare over for Sierra and Ben.

While the two uniforms went around back, Nash and Taylor approached the front entrance with SAPD Sergeant Baker holding the leash to a bomb-sniffing dog. Taylor held the screen open while Nash struck the door with a battering ram. The second time it burst open. After notifying the two in the backyard, the sergeant went in first, checking for any bomb traps. Nash notified the two in back that Baker was making his way through the house. Taylor moved inside with Nash closely following behind him.

Taylor went to the left with Baker and his K-9 partner down the hallway to the bedrooms. After letting the other two officers inside, Nash joined Taylor while the others checked the garage for Richardson.

When Taylor came to the last bedroom, the sight only reinforced that they had the right suspect. When Nash stood at his side, Taylor stared at all the pink and frills. "Richardson's preserved his daughter's bedroom for the past two years. He hasn't moved on."

"We need to canvass the neighborhood," Nash said. "I'll inform headquarters he isn't here. Maybe someone saw him or has a surveillance camera that might reveal when he left and how."

When they made their way back to the kitchen, one of the officers was waiting. "You might want to take a look at the car in the garage. It's the one stolen after the second shooting."

"Did you find a way into the attic?" Taylor asked the officers as he walked toward the garage.

"Yes, but we didn't find anyone up there. In fact, nothing was stored there."

While Nash stayed with Baker to call headquarters, Taylor stepped into the garage with the two officers. The stolen car sat a few feet away. He circled it, ending up peeking into the driver's side window. He opened the door. "There looks like a bloodstain on the seat." He popped the trunk and examined it, filled with items that were most likely the original owner's. "Go out to the backyard and thoroughly search it to make sure he didn't leave that way."

When Taylor returned to the kitchen, Nash disconnected his call and looked at him. "Forensics is on its way."

Taylor was puzzled. "We didn't find any bomb-making materials. Richardson might have another place, but how did he get away? The last car he stole is in the garage and the vehicle registered to him is in the driveway."

The sound of a dog barking out front drew Taylor into the living room with Nash right behind him. Baker's German shepherd was on alert by the trunk of Richardson's car.

"There's a bomb." Taylor ran out the door as Baker and his dog moved away from the area.

Sierra finished cleaning up after lunch. Taylor had been gone over an hour. She stared at the stainless-steel sink, chewing on her thumbnail, a habit she used to have when worry consumed her—not for her, because Robert and Dallas were here to protect Ben and her. But for Taylor. When he had told her he needed to follow through and be part of the raid on the suspect's home, she understood. This case had become personal for him, as well. If he hadn't reacted so quickly in her office, the bomb would have killed both of them.

She turned away from the sink and began pacing. Surely, they had raided the suspect's house by now. She wanted this over with. How could she and Ben move on with the killer still out there?

Why hadn't Taylor called to tell her what happened? What was going on at Richardson's house? Was there something she missed? She thought back to when her sister had been dealing with Charlene and her illness. A memory taunted her, but she couldn't quite grasp it.

So intense in thought, Sierra gasped when John appeared in the doorway.

"Sorry. I didn't mean to surprise you." John came into the kitchen.

"How did it go today?"

"Not well. How much does Ben know about the case?"

"I've tried to keep details from him. I don't

want him to worry and get any more upset than he is."

"You need to tell him some of what's going on. He drew a picture of you and Taylor sitting at the dining room table. Right after it, he started to tear it up. I stopped him. When I asked him about why he drew it, he pressed his lips together and sat on the floor with Oscar."

"I wish he would use his words. You think he knows something and is upset."

"Taylor is gone. Dallas is here. Do you think he knows about the raid on Richardson's house?"

As she ran her fingers through her hair, she thought back over the morning. "Maybe. It's hard to have a conversation with him. He doesn't respond."

"But he does. His facial expressions, drawings and gestures say a lot. I noticed your pacing. If you're worried about Taylor, it's possible Ben is, too."

"What do I do?"

"Tell him what's going on. Not in detail but let him know where Taylor is. Then try to take his mind off of it. You mentioned earlier to me that Dallas has a friend who has some puppies, and that Ben's going to pick one of them out soon. How about doing it today? Dallas can get a message to Taylor."

"Okay, if Dallas thinks it's safe." In that moment she realized she could use the distraction, too.

While waiting for the bomb squad to deal with the bomb, Taylor and Nash had the police officers cordon off the area around the car.

"We need to let the neighbors know and interview them about Richardson," Nash said. "I hope some are home right now."

Taylor nodded. "I'll take the other side of the street. I'll get two of the officers to help us."

Taylor started at the end of the block and worked his way toward the middle of it where Richardson's house was. Officer Perez began at the other end. When Taylor rang the doorbell of the house across from the suspect, he glimpsed Perez approaching the place two down from him. Taylor hoped the officer had leads because Taylor had come up empty-handed so far.

When no one came to the door, he knocked on it and glanced over his shoulder at the bomb squad dealing with some kind of device in the trunk of Richardson's car. He turned to leave but halted at the sound of someone unlocking the door.

An elderly man with a head of white hair stood in the entrance, looking past Taylor. "What's going on?"

"I'm Texas Ranger Taylor Blackburn. I just have a few questions for you."

"I'm Clyde Zoller." He leaned on his cane, his shoulder against the door frame.

Taylor showed him Richardson's photo. "Is this your neighbor across the street?"

"Yep. Why?"

"There's a bomb in the trunk of Max Richardson's car."

"Do I have to leave?"

"No, the bomb squad is dealing with it. Have you seen Richardson today?"

"Yep. Early this morning when he arrived home. I'm an early riser and always come outside on the porch and drink a cup of coffee. I've been doing it for the past twenty years."

"Did he go into his house?"

"Yes, but he left in a car not twenty minutes later."

"What kind of car?"

"Actually, a white pickup."

"Did you get the license plate number or make?"

Clyde shook his head.

"Do you know where he might have gone?"

"Nope. He hasn't said a word to me in the past two years. Just a few weeks ago, he walked right by me with his eyes downcast. He nearly knocked my cane out from under me. Thankfully I caught myself before going down. He wouldn't have helped me up."

"Does he have family around here or friends he might go see?"

Clyde's eyes widened. "He's the guy everyone is looking for, isn't he? I came in this morning at the end of a news broadcast. I only got a fuzzy glimpse of the picture. I didn't have my glasses on yet. Is that the same guy?"

"Yes."

"Do you know any of his friends or family?" Taylor asked again, impatient. He hated being gone too long from Sierra and Ben. When he'd left his dad's home earlier, he'd actually had hope that the case would be wrapped up today. He should have known better. He just hated seeing how afraid Sierra was while trying not to show it.

The older man rubbed his chin. "There used to be people coming and going from his house. That stopped when his daughter died. And then a month ago, his wife died, too. He got downright mean after that. He certainly is angry."

Taylor withdrew a card with his contact information on it and handed it to Clyde. "I'd love your help. Give me a call if you see Max Richardson."

"Will do. But I don't see him coming back. I said he was angry, but he's also intense and very smart."

"Thanks. That's good to know." Taylor noticed the police officer still at the other house two doors down. "Who's your neighbor?" He gestured toward the place next door, the last one to be canvassed.

"That's Nanny Bee. If there's anything you want to know about Max, she might know. She knows everything that goes on around here and loves to share with others. She loves to talk."

"Is she at home?"

"She's always there. She never leaves her house."

Taylor tipped his hat and left the front porch. "Good." He headed to Nanny Bee's home. Maybe she would have an idea where Richardson could have gone.

He rang the bell. According to Clyde, she was here. Maybe she didn't open the door to a stranger. "Ms. Nanny Bee," he called through the door, "I'm Texas Ranger Blackburn. Clyde told me you're home. I need to talk to you."

A couple of minutes later, the door opened a few inches.

"Where's your identification?" asked a woman in her seventies wearing a long terry cloth robe, her arms crossed over her chest.

He showed her his badge, and she parted the door a couple of more inches.

"What do you need? I was in the middle of a TV show I'd like to see."

He took out the photo and held it up. "Do you know who he is?"

"Max Richardson, although he's usually wearing glasses. Can't see much in front of him."

"Do you know where he is?"

"At his house. I haven't seen him leave."

She must not be as vigilant as Clyde thought. "No, he isn't home."

"I'm rarely wrong." With her forehead scrunched, she looked at him with doubt. "Is that why the police are at his house? Did something happen to him?"

"There was a bomb found in the trunk of his car. But he isn't at his house. Do you know anywhere he could be?"

The older woman shook her head. "I can't help you. Now, if you don't mind, I'd like to get back to my show."

She shut the door before Taylor could say anything. She must be really into that TV program.

As he walked across the street, he sensed someone watching him. He stopped and swung around. Clyde stood in the front window and waved to him.

The bomb squad was packing up to leave after they deactivated the bomb. He met Nash by his car and compared notes about what they heard from the people on the block. "The neighbors I talked to don't know where Richardson is. With him out there somewhere, I need to leave to pick up Sierra and Ben. I want to make sure they are protected. Can you come by my dad's tonight to go over the case?"

Nash nodded.

Taylor climbed into his rented SUV and headed toward the ranch. He'd wanted Richardson arrested today. Sierra and Ben had already gone through so much. He wanted their nightmare to end.

One thought intruded into his mind as he drove. What would it be like if he and Sierra had met under normal circumstances?

Sierra held Ben's hand as they walked with Dallas, Rachel Young, his fiancée, and Michelle, his daughter, to the barn on Rachel's father's ranch. Ben actually was tugging Sierra along because apparently she wasn't walking fast enough.

"C'mon, Ben. I'll race you to the barn," Michelle said.

Ben dropped Sierra's hand and raced toward the black building and reached the double doors before the teenager. He pivoted toward her with a huge grin on his face.

"Thank you, Rachel, for letting us come today," Sierra told the woman walking beside her. "I don't think I could have sat around Robert's house waiting to see what happened when Taylor and Nash went to arrest the suspect."

"I certainly understand. Besides, Dad is thrilled someone wants to adopt one of the puppies. He's taking more and more animals in, which means he needs more people to adopt them. People even leave abandoned animals at the ranch gate all the time."

Dallas slipped his arm along Rachel's shoulders. "Believe me, it's hard to refuse Bill when he asks. I've taken a few to care for. Michelle loves it. She even comes and helps Bill with the animals on the weekend."

When Sierra entered the barn, she spied her nephew in a small enclosure sitting on the ground as puppies crawled all over him. The smile hadn't left his face, especially when he tried to hold two wiggly dogs, both feverishly licking him.

"They've been weaned for a few days. Two males and two females. Ben, you can pick anyone you want," Rachel said when the group stopped on the other side of the pen.

He giggled when one snuggled against his ear.

While Sierra watched him play with each puppy, she kept checking her watch.

Dallas came to her side. "He can take care of himself. He'll be all right."

"I know. I just want this all over with and this man behind bars."

"Believe me, every law enforcement officer in the area is looking for this man."

"Waiting is hard to do."

Rachel leaned forward. "I've been on both ends of it. I'm the sheriff, so Dallas has had to wait for me and I have for him. Neither is fun."

"What kind of dog do you think these puppies are?" Sierra asked, needing to take the conversation away from what was happening with the hunt for Max Richardson.

"Not sure. The mother has a lot of corgi in

her. The father might have been one of the terrier breeds."

Ben finally stood up with a brown-and-white
puppy in his arms. He brought him to Rachel.

"Is this the one you want?"

He nodded.

"Then he's yours." Rachel looked at Sierra.
"Are you taking him today?"

Before Sierra could answer, Ben looked between her and Rachel, then took off running toward the open barn doors, cuddling the puppy
against his chest. Heart racing, Sierra whirled
around, ready to defend her nephew. Instead,
relief trembled through her when she saw who
stood there.

"Yes, we're taking the puppy today." Taylor
entered the barn, looking tired and worn out.
But alive!

She headed toward Taylor as Ben showed him
the puppy he picked.

Taylor knelt in front of Ben and took the dog
from him, holding the puppy up. "What are you
going to name him?"

Ben's lower lip stuck out while he looked up
in deep thought.

"Tell you what, Ben. It took me some time
before I decided on Oscar's name. You should
think about it for a while."

Ben nodded and took the puppy from Taylor.

Dallas, Rachel and Michelle joined them at the entrance.

"I've got some Christmas cookies and hot chocolate waiting for y'all at the house. Want some?" Michelle asked Ben.

Ben started out for the house. Michelle quickly followed.

"I'll let y'all discuss the case. I'll catch up with them." Rachel took off after Ben and Michelle.

When they were out of earshot, Taylor turned his back on the house and faced Dallas and Sierra. "Richardson has left his house. We haven't found him yet. I interviewed some of the neighbors. According to one, Richardson wasn't home and had been gone since early this morning. He thought it was strange that he left his car and drove away in a pickup that the man across the street hadn't seen before. I showed the man the picture we have of our suspect, and he identified Max Richardson."

"Any indication where Richardson went?" Dallas asked.

Taylor shook his head. "Richardson used to be social with his neighbors, but ever since his daughter died, he kept to himself and his wife.

But since she died a month ago, the neighbors have hardly seen him."

"His wife's death could have been his trigger." Dallas adjusted his cowboy hat.

"I'd say definitely. I checked on her death on my way here. She committed suicide."

"Are the police sure it was a suicide?" Dallas asked.

"Yes, she was visiting her mom in Austin. She left a note, then took sleeping pills."

While Sierra listened to them discuss the wife's death, a chilly wind swept through her. The killer was still out there, possibly planning more. Now she could only hope his photo being splashed all over the news would lead to his capture. "So, what do we do now?"

"Follow the leads. The tip line has been busy. The police are following up on all credible tips. We'll dig into his past. Interview people who know him. He'll make a mistake." Taylor turned toward the house. "We need to leave. I want to be back at Dad's before dark."

Sierra walked between the two Texas Rangers to the kitchen door. When she entered the home, the scent of chocolate filled the air. Ben sat by Michelle at a table for six, stuffing a cookie into his mouth, then washing it down with a swallow of hot chocolate that left a brown moustache over his upper lip. In front of him was a piece of paper he'd been drawing on while Michelle was doing the same thing, her pencil moving quickly over the sheet.

Rachel approached Sierra. "Michelle suggested they draw a picture of the puppies. And they've been doing that since coming in here, only stopping long enough to have a bite of a cookie and a drink of hot chocolate. Why don't we take ours into the living room?"

"We can't stay too long, but I hate ending this," Sierra replied. The smile on Ben's face as he drew his picture and petted his new puppy curled on his lap gave Sierra hope that her nephew would be all right with time.

After Nash left later that evening, Taylor pored over any information he could find on Max Richardson for the second time. Still nothing about where he could have gone. Nor was there anything at his house to indicate a hiding place. As the neighbors had said and others who knew Richardson had corroborated, he had withdrawn from all his friends and had even lost his job six weeks before the shooting. The police were now worried that the killer would next attack the grocery store where he'd been an assistant manager. Nash had contacted the place of business about his concerns.

Taylor had gone through Richardson's bank and credit card records, as well as the call log on the cell phone he'd left on his kitchen table. But he'd come up with nothing of import. His car was too old to track its GPS to see where he'd gone in the past weeks. He didn't own property other than his house the police had scoured for evidence. But they'd found nothing. Only the car had yielded any evidence. Not only was a bomb in the trunk but so were some bomb-making ingredients. Nash was tracking down friends and associates, and Taylor hoped the lieutenant would find a lead to Richardson's whereabouts because he was coming up with nothing useful on his end.

He stood and stretched. He'd been sitting for hours. He needed to move around. Perhaps that would help him connect the dots with all the information he'd collected about Richardson. He walked into the kitchen to refill his mug.

As he poured his coffee, he wondered if Richardson was finished with his vengeance. Had he slipped through the dragnet they had around San Antonio, and was he already states away? His photo had made national TV news. Someone out there might know something about where he was. Many other criminals had been apprehended because of a tip from the public.

As Taylor turned from the counter, Ben stood in front of him with his puppy in his arms and Oscar next to him. The boy pointed at the door.

"You think both of them need to go outside?"

Ben nodded.

"Then let's go." Taylor crossed to the back door and opened it.

Ben stepped outside and put his unnamed puppy on the ground. Oscar nudged the dog, then trotted a few yards away with the pup following.

"Oscar is a good role model for your pet. Are you still thinking of a name? He's going to need one."

Ben nodded again.

"Having a pet is a big responsibility. You're going to do a good job."

Oscar headed back toward them with Ben's dog running to keep up. The boy scooped up his puppy, and they all returned to the house.

Sierra was next to the refrigerator, waiting for them. "It's time to put your pet into his crate. Until he's house trained, he can't sleep with you. Remember, that's why we bought a crate for him. He has bedding in there."

Ben frowned.

The child hadn't been happy at the pet store they had stopped at on the way back to this house. Taylor ruffled his hair. "You still have Oscar."

Ben plodded to the crate and put the puppy inside.

"Let's go. It's past your bedtime." Sierra clasped his shoulder and guided him toward the door.

"Ben, tomorrow we'll play fetch outside with both of them." Taylor watched them leave the kitchen, and then he snatched up his mug and returned to the dining room.

He retook his chair and stared at the computer, wondering if going through the information on Richardson for a third time would help. He felt like he was missing something, and yet he couldn't figure it out. Frustration churned his stomach.

"Ben is finally asleep, I think because I told him the faster he goes to bed the faster tomorrow morning will come and he can see his pet."

Taylor glanced over his shoulder and smiled at Sierra. "That's good. We probably should take that advice, too. Tomorrow will be a busy day."

Sierra sat in the chair catty-corner from Taylor, looked at the computer and sighed.

"I think we both need a break from staring at

the screen. One good thing came out of today. We know who the shooter is and most likely the reason."

She folded her arms over her chest. "There is no justification for what that man did. We did what we could. I looked at the bills the Richardsons received. Kat stopped charging him even the copayments for those last months. She did that for people who were struggling to pay their medical bills."

Taylor came to his feet and held out his hand. "Let's sit on the couch and look at the Christmas tree lights and unwind before we call it a day. We can start back tomorrow morning."

In the living room, Sierra cuddled next to Taylor. They kept the room dark, lit only by the twinkling tree lights. "There's something calming about only the Christmas tree lights being on. It reminds me of God being the light in the dark, showing us the way."

"I like the quiet and peace. It's been a hectic day."

"A hectic week. So much has happened in a short time."

Taylor slid his arm around Sierra, thinking about all that had occurred and how it was altering him. There was one big change. For the first time since his wife died, he was attracted to a woman. "When the case is solved, and I intend for it to be soon, I don't want to lose contact with you."

For a few seconds Sierra tensed, then pulled back. "I've mentioned how Kat saved me going down the wrong path when I was teenager, but I never told you why I did it. What triggered my anger and rebellion."

In the soft lighting from the tree, Taylor could see concern in her eyes. She moved back a few inches as though to distance herself. Her gaze fell on a spot between them on the couch.

"When I was twelve, my sister was dating this guy in college. Kat was eight years older than me and also buried in her books or working to earn enough to feed us and put a roof over our heads. I was still mourning Mom. I don't think Kat ever got a chance to. She became more a mother to me than a big sis." Sierra pressed her lips together and stared at the twinkling lights on the tree, opening and closing her hands.

Taylor felt compassion surge within him. "As you know I've gone through losing two important people in my life in the past nine years. I've learned that people grieve in different ways. Filling the role of mother for you when you needed it might have helped Kat through her grief. And as for you, well, being a teenager is a roller-coaster trip. You're going through the transition from child to adult. It can be a challenge for anyone."

"So much of what you said, Kat did, too. But at twelve, thirteen and fourteen, I wasn't listening." Sierra leaned against the arm of the couch, bringing her legs up and clasping them against her chest. "I was angry—at Mom dying, at life, at..." She looked away, swallowing hard. "You wouldn't understand."

The pain he heard in her voice touched him. Staring at her, he could see brick by brick a wall being constructed between them. His gut twisted into a tight knot. "There's very little you could tell me that would shock me. I've seen the best and the worst of humankind in my job."

"I couldn't even tell Kat the whole story. I tried to, but the words would never come out." Tears shone in her eyes.

And broke his heart.

She scrambled off the couch and stood, a rivulet of sorrow coursing down her cheeks. "I need to get to bed. Tomorrow will be a long day." She whirled around and started toward the staircase.

He couldn't let her go like that—hurting, crying for help. He hurried after her. At the bottom of the steps, he said, "Wait, Sierra... Please don't go."

* * *

Don't go. The plea in Taylor's voice halted her in midstride. Sierra placed her foot on the stair and slowly rotated toward him, a few steps away from her. Across the space, his gaze connected with hers, holding her in place as he came closer. The appeal in his eyes pleaded for an explanation.

Earlier she'd set out to tell him something she hadn't shared with others—only with God. She didn't want any secrets between them, and yet she didn't know if she could say it out loud. The repulsiveness and self-loathing the memories always produced didn't happen this time as she looked into Taylor's caring expression.

"Do you really think you can go to sleep? If you don't want to share it with me, that's okay. It's your choice. But right now, you're so wound up."

"It's Kat's death. I can usually shove it back in the box and not think about it. I can't anymore and now I know why. For years, a part of me has blamed my sister for what happened. Until a few minutes ago, I didn't really realize that."

Taylor held out his hand.

She stared at it for a long moment, then placed hers in his and came down the stairs. Her heartbeat thumped against her chest.

Back in the living room, Taylor flipped on a light on the table next to the couch, then took a seat at the opposite end from Sierra. "I'd like to sit next to you, but I'm not going to unless you want me to. You're struggling with something, and I want to be there for you, but you tell me what you want."

She shook her head. "I should never have started this conversation."

"Who hurt you?"

"Why do you say that?"

"I can hear it in your voice."

And no doubt saw it on her face, where she wore her emotions, especially lately. She'd started this conversation, and she needed to finish it. She inhaled a composing breath. "I was twelve when it happened, not too long after my mother died. As I said before, Kat had been dating a guy she went to college with. The relationship became serious and Brent was around all the time. The first time he came over, when Kat was supposed to be home but was running late, he molested me. He scared me and threatened me. I was dealing with my mother's death and didn't know what to do. Kat was all I had, and she loved Brent. I believed him when he said he would hurt me and my sister if I said anything. He was big and muscular." Once the words started, she wanted to complete the story. She moved down the couch and sat next to Taylor, his presence a soothing balm to her memories. She covered his hand on the couch between them. "After that, I was never around when he was until he surprised me a few months later."

Taylor tensed, his jawline rigid like a piece of granite.

"I kicked and fought him any way I could. I got loose and ran away. I was so frightened he would find me. Once I tried calling my sister, but Brent answered the phone. It was summer, so I lived on the streets. As much as I missed Kat, I wasn't going to go back. Then I was caught by the police. Kat had reported me missing. She came to pick me up alone. As she took me home, I intended to leave again if Brent came around, but the words about what he had done wouldn't come out."

"What happened when you returned home?" Tension weaved its way through his words and expression.

"Kat had spent so much of what little off time she had looking for me. Brent got tired of it and broke up with her. I kept what Brent did inside me. While I watched my sister mourn the loss of him, I celebrated it. Kat concentrated on her schoolwork, which had suffered while I was gone for a month. When she wasn't studying, she was at her job. And while that was going on, I retreated further from her. I was glad she was so busy that she didn't date anyone else. Then she met her future husband, who just wanted me gone. He had no interest in me. When they married, I was seventeen. I stayed at a girlfriend's house more than I did with Kat and Kalvin. At the community college I went to, I dated occasionally but could never relax totally around a man."

Until Taylor.

"What happened when Kalvin left Kat?"

"It devastated her. She was pregnant, and he didn't want a child. Kalvin left not long after Ben was born. I moved back in with her to help with Ben. I wanted to tell her about Brent then, but she told me how lousy she was at picking a man. I'd never seen my sister vulnerable. I knew then I wasn't going to add to her problems. It was behind me, or so I thought. Now I know I should have spoken up."

"You just did to me. The more you talk about it the more you work your way through the trauma. I'll listen anytime."

She smiled. "Thanks."

"I know I wouldn't be where I am today if I hadn't turned to John for help."

"The same goes for Ben. He needs to talk about what he's going through. As you and I know, keeping it inside doesn't make it go away. John hopes he will, but there's no guarantee. All I can do now is be there for him, love him and pray for him."

"Earlier today, I thought he would speak out with a name for his new puppy. I could see it in his face. He even opened his mouth, then slowly closed it. I think it'll happen when we can tell him the shooter is in jail, when he won't be so afraid. Now at least we know who he is and what his motive is. He put in motion his revenge when his wife committed suicide. He's lost his family, and he had to blame someone."

At the mention of the killer, still at large, Sierra stood, nervous energy running through her. She skirted the table and paced. She felt like a boiling pan of water with the lid on. Steam leaked out, but what would happen when the top was removed?

Taylor stepped into her path. "Right now, it might look like this will never end, but it will. Richardson will be caught. And then your life will start to return to normal, and Ben will learn to deal with his emotions." He held her gaze as he came closer. "I still want to stay in contact with you. See you. Nothing you've said has changed that."

When he closed the space between them, she stayed where she was. He cupped her elbows and slowly drew her even closer. Her lips tingled with anticipation as he leaned toward her. This time he kissed her with no hesitation, tugging her flat against him. She locked her arms around him and relished the moment.

Not a word was said when Taylor pulled back and slung his arm along her shoulder and pressed her against his side. She looked up at the Christmas tree, at the big star on the top, and she thought about the hope that star in the sky over Bethlehem had given the people below. Seeing this one offered her that hope, too.

A blanket of peace enfolded her.

Until the house alarm blared through the quiet air.

TEN

Taylor wrenched away from Sierra and withdrew his gun. "Hide behind the couch."

As Sierra crawled into the small space between the sofa and wall, he quickly checked the front entrance, then moved down the hallway toward the other entry point, the kitchen. Adrenaline surged through him, his heart pumping fast. He flattened himself against the wall and peered into the room.

Trembling, Ben stood in the doorway to the backyard. He held his puppy, while Oscar stood next to the frightened boy. Eyes wide, he looked at Taylor.

He rushed to Ben and drew him away while Taylor shut the door. "Stay right here."

Taylor hurried into the entryway and punched in the code to stop the piercing sound.

His dad was halfway down the staircase when quiet reigned in the house again. "What happened?"

"Ben tried to go outside. Everything's all right."

His father continued down the stairs as Sierra came out of the living room.

"Why was Ben going outside?" She looked toward the kitchen and hurried to Ben. "Why were you leaving the house?"

Her nephew didn't say anything.

Sierra clasped her arms around him, throwing her glance at Taylor.

He came to stand beside them. "Were you taking your pet outside to go to the bathroom?"

Eyes still big, Ben nodded.

"Because you wanted to take him upstairs with you?"

Ben gave another nod.

"Tell you what. Let's take the crate upstairs to your room, so he'll be in there with you. Okay?"

Ben's answer was a big smile.

"You've got to remember the alarm is on at all times."

Ben dipped his head and rubbed his cheek against his puppy.

Taylor went into the utility room, picked up the crate and returned to Ben. "While we're here, let's take our dogs outside."

"Sounds good. I'll take the crate upstairs and go back to sleep," Robert said.

Taylor handed it to his father, then headed to

the back door with Ben on one side and Sierra on the other. "We'll be quick, and we won't go far from the patio."

As Ben put his puppy down in the grass nearby and Oscar wandered off, Sierra hugged her arms against her. "Did you purposely forget to mention grabbing coats?" She shivered next to Taylor.

He grinned at her, the outside patio light illuminating her beautiful face. "This isn't cold to me." He leaned close and lowered his voice. "But yes, you're right."

"I figured as much."

Taylor wound his arms around her. "Does that help?"

"Yes."

Oscar trotted back as Ben scooped up his puppy and dashed for the back door.

Sierra quickly followed while Taylor paused at the entrance, his gaze sweeping the landscape. When he threw the dead bolt lock into place, he breathed a little easier.

After he reset the alarm, they took Ben to his room. The child placed his pet in the crate, then hopped into bed. He pointed at the air mattress Sierra had been sleeping on near the bed, then waved his hand toward the door.

"Is this your way of telling me you don't need

me to stay in here anymore?" she asked while tucking Ben in for the night.

He grinned.

"Okay. I'll return to the room across the hall." Sierra kissed her nephew's cheek, then straightened. "No more middle-of-the-night trips outside."

Ben nodded.

The night-light in the room gave off enough illumination for Sierra to make her way around the air mattress and into the corridor. She pulled the door almost closed except for a foot-wide gap.

Sierra crossed the hall to her bedroom, where she'd left her belongings. "I think having his own dog was the best move we could do for him."

"I agree," Taylor said. "I wasn't sure the timing was good when Dallas called about going to the ranch earlier, but I'm glad he did. While we're gone tomorrow, he'll be focused on his puppy. Maybe he'll come up with a name soon."

"It's an important job when naming a pet."

"Has he ever had a pet?"

"A goldfish and gerbil. Kat was working him up to taking care of a dog. He did a such good job cleaning out the gerbil cage that when it died, Kat decided to get him a puppy for Christmas." When Sierra yawned, she quickly covered her mouth.

"Bored already?"

"Funny. No, but I'm tired. Good night." She put her hand on the doorknob and turned it, but he stopped her.

"Sierra, thanks for sharing tonight."

She smiled over her shoulder, a gleam in her eyes.

That look struck him in the heart. In a short time, he felt he knew her better than people he'd been friends with for years. Nah, that couldn't be right. He could read people, but to say they knew each other well wasn't possible—not in less than a week, even if it was an intense five days. He'd shared more with her than anyone. Even when he talked with John after his son died, it had taken a while to break down his walls. But not with Sierra.

Taylor shook his head. This kind of thinking wasn't good. His job was to protect her and Ben and find the killer. He couldn't do that with her always dominating his thoughts. If anything happened to Sierra because of him, he'd never forgive himself.

A slash of sunlight speared her coverlet as Sierra sat up in bed. She'd slept the best she had in a long time. Probably from sheer exhaustion, she reasoned. It certainly wasn't because she shared her past with Taylor.

She bent over, burying her face in her hands. Why did she do that? Once the police found the killer, she and Taylor would probably drift apart. She needed to put her life back together as well as Ben's, and put her home in order. She would have to be strong for Ben. They had only each other—and the Lord.

She climbed from the bed and changed into a sweatshirt and pants. They still didn't know where Max Richardson was hiding. Maybe there was something they were missing. She'd seen the coverage he was getting. And she knew that surveillance cameras that could pick him up were everywhere.

Sierra left her room and crossed the hall to peek into Ben's. She inched the door open wider. With Oscar next to him, her nephew sat on the bed, holding his puppy up. Ben's mouth was moving as though he were whispering something to his dog. She started to enter and see if he would talk to her, but she held back. She remembered once when Taylor had said he would talk to Oscar but not others about what he was feeling. That it had taken a while for him to open up to John. When Ben was ready, he would talk to her. Trying to force him wouldn't work, and it could possibly even make the situation worse.

She straightened and headed downstairs, where she caught sight of Taylor at the dining room table. "Did you get any sleep last night?"

He glanced back at her and smiled. "Yes, all of three hours. I kept running through what happened yesterday at Richardson's house. It was Saturday, and there were about half his neighbors home. I'd like to go back and talk with a couple of them at least who lived near Richardson and maybe catch some others at their houses. One of them might know where he would go. Dallas will be here. Nash and his officers are stretched pretty thin, what with the funeral taking place today. He has an officer at Richardson's house."

"Let's go by before the funeral. I can stay in the car or with the SAPD officer."

"We have a few hours before that. I've been checking all the traffic cams in the area to see if I can spot him."

"I can help. I need to do something." Sierra walked toward the kitchen. "I smelled coffee. Do you need a refill?"

"Nope. Just got one before you came down. As soon as Ben is up, Dad will make breakfast."

She paused in the entrance into the kitchen, spying Robert at the table reading a paper. "He's up and I think I caught him talking to his puppy. He didn't know I was there. I didn't say anything to him, but I should go up there and make sure the dogs go outside."

Robert stood. "I'll go. Maybe he would like to help me make breakfast."

Sierra grinned. "Are you sure? He helped me a couple of times, and the mess to clean up afterward was twice as much as usual."

"I'm not worried. We'll take the dogs out first, then cook. You and Taylor find Richardson."

Sierra poured coffee into her mug, then returned to the dining room and sat in front of her computer.

"I sent you some footage to look at. If you see anyone who looks like Richardson, not just the driver, let me know."

Sierra stared at the screen, pausing it occasionally to assess each person in a car. Being a law enforcement officer, she was learning, wasn't all action. In fact, a lot of it was tedious. So much of her job was with the computer, and so was Taylor's.

Ben charged down the stairs and ran into the living room with his puppy in his arms and

Oscar behind him. He breezed by Taylor and her and into the kitchen. She was grateful she didn't have to hide what was on her computer screen.

Sierra entered the funeral home with Taylor right beside her. The bulletproof vest he'd insisted she wear felt awkward. Her light coat helped to camouflage it, but the fact she had it on only reinforced she was a possible target for Richardson.

Taylor escorted her to Mindy's family in an anteroom before the funeral started. "As soon as the service is over," he told her as they walked, "we'll need to leave. I want you in the car before it's dark."

Sierra greeted Mr. and Mrs. Carson with a hug. "Thank you for inviting me to join you before the service."

Mrs. Carson held Sierra's hands. "You didn't need to come. I would have understood."

"I know. I need to say goodbye to Mindy. I still can't believe all that has happened this week."

Tears filled Mrs. Carson's eyes. "I know what you mean. I feel like I'm living a nightmare, and I just need to wake up and everything will be fine."

"I wish. Mindy was my best friend. Losing

her and…" Sierra couldn't finish the sentence. Grief jammed her throat. She quickly leaned in and gave Mindy's mother another hug, finally saying, "I'll miss her every day."

"Me, too."

Someone working for the funeral home approached Mindy's parents.

"Don't be a stranger," Mrs. Carson said to Sierra before the staff member stopped in front of Mr. Carson.

Taylor put his arm around her and headed for the door. "Nash has saved us a place at the back."

When she entered the chapel, she said, "I want to view Mindy. I appreciate they arranged some time with the family before the funeral."

Taylor positioned himself behind Sierra in the line to pass the coffin. He kept one hand at the small of her back while he scanned the crowd. She knew that the man stationed at the head of the casket was a plainclothes police officer, identified by the US flag on his lapel.

"Are you all right?" Taylor whispered in her ear when only two people separated her from the casket.

"No." Again her throat clogged up, and she swallowed several times. She still had to go through the other funerals, especially Kat's.

How was she going to hold herself together for Ben?

One day at a time. God will be with me. I'm not alone.

When she got her first glimpse of Mindy's face, so peaceful, tears welled up into her eyes, and she could hardly make out her features.

Taylor handed her a tissue.

She turned her head toward him. "How did you know?" She dabbed at the wet tracks running down her face.

"Your body language."

"I didn't want to cry in front of everyone."

"Don't hold in the sorrow. It's good to release it. I didn't, and I should have, especially with TJ."

His soft words reassured her she wasn't alone. She clung to them, realizing he'd been there twice.

When she stood in front of the casket and looked down at Mindy, memories of all the times they had spent together paraded across her mind. Good memories filled with laughter and friendship. Mindy was with the Lord now, and He would take care of her.

As Taylor escorted her to the back pew, where Nash was, she swept the crowd, seeing other friends of Mindy's. She wished she could stay and talk to some of them, but even her coming was a risk. She never wanted to be the reason someone else was hurt. Earlier, unknown to most, the chapel and funeral home had been swept for bombs. She felt better knowing that.

After the family filed in and paid their last respects to Mindy, the service began. In the photos of Mindy's life shown on a big screen, Sierra was often in them. She bit her lower lip to keep from crying, not always successful, but Taylor was there to hold her hand and give her tissues.

At the end of the service, she slanted a look at him and realized she was falling deeper in love with him.

"We need to leave now." Taylor took her hand and rose, then led the way out of the pew and chapel.

In the lobby a uniformed police officer hurried up to Taylor. "I just heard the hotel next door is evacuating. A bomb threat. It's mass confusion. The crowds are swarming all around."

"Thanks for letting me know."

"A bomb. Is this Max's doing?" Sierra asked when the officer went back outside where he was posted.

"Possibly."

Nash came out of the chapel, a frown marring his face. "The funeral director just found me and said he got a call about a bomb on the premises. We're evacuating this building even though it was swept an hour ago for bombs."

"The same thing is happening at the hotel next door. This is Richardson." Taylor still held her hand and started forward. "We need to get her out of here and to a safe place. Richardson could be anywhere."

Nash pointed at an exit door. "This way." As he led them to the door, he spoke into his comm. "We'll need support. Keep an eye out for Max Richardson. He could be anywhere. We're going out the far-right door."

Sierra glanced over her shoulder at the near-empty atrium. She could hardly drag in a decent breath as her heart thudded rapidly and seemed to expand to encompass her whole chest.

The doors opened to the chapel, and people flooded out into the lobby. A wall of people raced for the exits.

Taylor slowed near the door, inspecting the area outside. Three police officers were nearby in the midst of a mob surging away from the hotel. "Stay close. Don't let go. The crowd might help us get away without Richardson seeing us. Nash, a police officer parked my car in the convention center lot across the street and was going to get it for me afterward, but that's not possible now. I don't even see the guy in the crowd."

"I'll be right behind you. We'll use my car. It's nearby."

When Taylor opened the door, a sea of people outside pressed against it in their rush to escape the bomb threat. Sierra and Nash helped to widen the gap, so they could get out. A surge of others behind them squashed Sierra up against Taylor. He wedged his body in the small space and shoved the crowd back enough to slip free with Sierra right behind him, then Nash.

Over the noise of the sirens and people around them, Nash shouted, "We need to go to the back lot."

Someone slammed against Sierra, sending her into Taylor. She grasped him as her feet went out from under her. Taylor tightened his grip on her to steady her while Nash used his body to protect her. Finally, she gained her footing while still moving forward with the mob.

As Sierra headed for the side of the funeral home, she felt like a salmon swimming upstream. A salmon with a target on its back. A big, burly man treaded on her foot, but despite the twinge that shot up her leg, she gritted her teeth and kept going.

Rounding the building, Taylor slowed and clasped Sierra against his side. "Nash, you take the lead. You know where your car is."

On this side of the funeral home, the mass of people dissipated. But Sierra was aware that they were still too close to the building. If there was a bomb, it could go off anytime, and there was a strong possibility they wouldn't survive. Their pace picked up, and she leaned into Taylor the more the pain in her foot intensified. She hurried as fast as she could, trying to ignore it. Taylor readjusted his arm around her to support more of her weight.

As Nash went around the funeral home to the back parking lot away from the river walk, he stopped for a few seconds as he surveyed the area.

"What happened?" Taylor gestured toward Sierra's foot.

"Someone stepped on it. I'm okay."

Nash waved them forward. "Black SUV in the second row."

Sierra came around the corner, being as alert as Taylor and Nash of her surroundings. A stream of people from the hotel crossed the parking lot as well as others from the funeral home.

Crack!

Taylor pushed her back around the corner while withdrawing his gun. The bullet ricocheted off the brick wall while another shot quickly followed the first. As she put her full weight on her hurt foot, it gave out, and before Taylor could stop her fall, she went down onto the sidewalk. Her head hit the concrete at the same time a piercing pain slashed through her flesh.

ELEVEN

"Sierra is down," Taylor shouted as Nash pulled the trigger on his gun.

A third shot coming from across the street reverberated through the air.

Using his body as a shield, Taylor moved Sierra out of the line of fire. He quickly called 911, apprising them of the situation with an active shooter and requesting an ambulance.

Nash moved to where Taylor was with Sierra, using the building as a shield. "I've called for backup and told them the direction the shots were coming from. I saw some police officers heading that way."

"Go with them. An ambulance is on its way. I want this guy caught today."

While Nash took off, Taylor assessed Sierra's injuries—a bump on the head, a gunshot wound in the left arm and an injured foot. He took out a handkerchief, which he'd brought in case Sierra had needed something more than a tissue at the funeral, and pressed it over the wound on her arm to stop the bleeding.

One of the police officers who had been out in front of the funeral home ran toward him.

"Lieutenant wanted me to help you."

"There's an ambulance on the way. It should be here at any moment. Direct them back here and keep people from coming around this side."

"Yes, sir."

Sierra's eyes fluttered open as the sound of a siren coming closer resonated through the air.

"Sierra, help is on the way. The shooting has stopped."

Trying to rise up, she moaned. She winced and sank back against Taylor's hand that cushioned the back of her head against the concrete. She licked her lips. "It hurts."

"You'll be all right. An ambulance is almost here."

She tried to smile, but it faded instantly. "Too much longer—" she closed her eyes for a few seconds, then lifted her eyelids halfway "—I'll know all the EMTs."

"Not if I have a say in it."

The police officer from earlier escorted the paramedics to Sierra. While they worked on her and prepared her for transportation to the hospital, Taylor continually watched the terrain around them. He hoped that Nash and the others caught Richardson. This had to end. Today.

What was it about Sierra that made the man so determined to finish the task of killing her? Had he totally lost it with his wife's suicide? Or was there a reason he couldn't let her get away?

While Sierra slept in her hospital bed, Taylor was looking through more security footage with his computer his dad brought him. This time the video feed was from around the funeral home. Richardson had slipped away from Nash and the other police looking for him. How did he get away undetected? The River Walk was crowded, especially with the hotel and funeral home being emptied of people.

His cell phone rang, and Taylor quickly answered it.

"Each building was inspected from top to bottom. No bombs were found," Nash said, working the crime scene along the river walk. "How's Sierra?"

"The doctors took care of her arm. She has a bad concussion and bruised foot from some guy stepping on it. She'll be staying at least a day, possibly two, depending how her head wound is."

"I'll keep you informed. Is a police officer standing guard?"

"Yes, but I'm not leaving tonight. There's a lounge chair I can use to sleep in, if I can sleep at all. Right now, I'm going through the footage. Richardson's picture has been plastered everywhere, and we haven't had a good tip yet. I have a theory. I think he's changed his appearance enough that it will be hard to tell it's him. Maybe something on the security video will help me find what he has done."

"I'll see you tomorrow unless something important comes up."

Taylor disconnected the call and stared at the far wall as he contemplated his theory. Changed his appearance how? Something in Richardson's background nagged Taylor. He opened the file he had on Richardson. He skimmed the man's history and found what was needling him. Richardson went to college and majored in electrical engineering. He also minored in theater. Too late to call the college, but first thing tomorrow morning, he would. What were the classes he took? Anything in makeup and special effects? So far, he'd been using his best facial recognition software to find Richardson in all the footage he'd been looking at. He needed to consider everything. Not just facial features but height, build, how he walked, mannerisms. He needed to get videos of Richardson to study the whole person.

Taylor went through another thirty minutes of tape, fighting sleep the whole way. Finally, he closed the computer and set it on a chair, then crossed to Sierra, who was sleeping. She looked so vulnerable. He should have been able to protect her. He pulled up a chair next to the bed and sat. He laid his hand over hers, relishing the connection. If he could trade places with her, he would. She'd been through so much.

In time, his eyelids grew heavy until he couldn't ignore his exhaustion any longer. Bending over, he kissed her cheek, then made his way to the lounger. The minute he settled into the chair his eyes slid shut, and the blackness swallowed him…

The mob swept Sierra forward toward Richardson, waiting with his gun aimed at her. Taylor watched from the sidelines as the shooter squeezed off three shots. A weight held Taylor in place for a few seconds, and when he finally moved, it was in slow motion, as though others were holding him back. The crowd vanished as she collapsed onto the sidewalk. He tried to reach her, but she was always just out of his grasp. All he could focus on was Sierra staring

at him, confused and in pain. Suddenly Rich-
ardson appeared above her, and he pointed his
weapon at her head. The bullet left the gun as
though time was being stretched out, but still
Taylor couldn't reach her. The shot struck her
forehead.

No!

Heart pounding, gasping for air, Taylor bolted straight up in the chair. For a few seconds he was confused about where he was. Sweat ran down his face, stinging his eyes as he stared at Sierra in the hospital bed. Alive.

He had to distance himself from Sierra. Now, before he fell in lo—

He shook his head. He'd almost not come back from the despair of losing his wife and son. He would *not* go through a third person he loved dying on him.

Sierra opened her eyes to bright sunlight streaming through the slats in the blinds covering the hospital window. When Dallas came into focus, she blinked. "What time is it?"

The Texas Ranger glanced at his watch. "Nine o'clock."

The jackhammer thudding against her skull made her brain fuzzy. "Monday?"

"Yes."

"Can you close the blinds? It's too bright in here." She ran her tongue over her parched lips and reached toward the table next to the bed for the plastic cup. Her hand shook as she drank the water.

After taking care of the blinds, Dallas approached her. "Here, I can help you." He took the cup. "Do you want more water?"

"No. I'm fine. Where's Taylor?" He told her he would make sure she was protected. She had expected him to be here when she woke up this morning. Was he okay? She couldn't remember everything that happened at the funeral home.

"He had a lead he wanted to track down, but he didn't want to leave you alone without someone in the room."

"I thought he said there was a police officer guarding the door."

"There is."

"How's Ben?"

"He's all right. Besides Robert, Ben's being protected by a deputy outside the house and one inside."

There was something she should remember, but it was just out of reach of her mind. Something about yesterday when she was brought to the hospital. The more she tried to recall it, the more her head hurt.

She closed her eyes, trying to picture what happened. A sound like firecrackers going off, followed by pain lancing through her. That was all she could remember. "When's Taylor going to be back?"

"I don't know. I've only been here for an hour."

"Does Ben know I'm in the hospital?"

"All Robert told Ben was that you and Taylor would be returning later today."

"If the doctor gives me the okay."

The door swished open, and a young nurse came into the room. "How are you feeling?"

"I've had better days."

The nurse smiled. "I imagine you have." She handed her a small cup with two pills in it. "You need to take these. It'll help your headache."

"How did you know my head felt as though it was split wide open?"

"Just a hunch. Dr. Nail will be here later this morning to check on you." The nurse showed her the button. "Use this if you need me."

As the woman turned to leave, Sierra asked, "Where am I?"

"Lone Star Hospital."

As she watched the door close behind the nurse, the name of the hospital plagued her. Why? She'd worked with several hospitals as the office/insurance manager for the clinic. What was the significance of this one?

Gotcha!

Taylor sat at his desk in his office at the Texas Ranger Headquarters in San Antonio and stared at the photo he believed was Max Richardson in disguise as he headed toward a car near the River Walk, not far from the funeral home. Leaning forward, Taylor watched as the shooter opened the trunk and put a duffel bag into it.

After spending hours watching Richardson's videos and going through his pictures Taylor felt he knew how the man walked with a slight limp, favoring his right leg. But also in two videos, he noticed that Richardson squinted when he took his tinted glasses off as though light hurt his eyes, which meant when being outside, the man definitely didn't like bright sunlight. And yesterday had been sunny.

When Richardson, dressed as an older man wearing dark sunglasses with hunched shoulders to diminish his height and a potbelly to disguise his thin physique, stepped away from the truck, Taylor got a good look at the license plate. He jotted down the number and then ran it through the DMV database.

When Clyde Zoller's name popped up, a coldness blanketed him. Had it been Richardson at the house across the street when he'd canvassed the neighborhood the other day? He closed his eyes and tried to recall meeting the older gentleman.

He withdrew his pad where he jotted down impressions and information from each interview. The minute he read the description of the old man, he knew it was the real Clyde Zoller. No amount of slouching could have put Richardson down to the height of five feet six inches.

Richardson hadn't been impersonating Clyde at that time, but had he been in the house when Taylor talked to Clyde? Or did he come back and steal his neighbor's car? Was Richardson at the man's home now? Was Clyde still alive?

The questions echoed in his mind, but Taylor had no answers. He should have gone back to the neighborhood and followed up with the people yesterday, but he couldn't let Sierra attend the funeral without him. Instead he'd sent two police officers who didn't find out any new information. He flipped through their report and noticed that no one answered at Clyde's house. He didn't have a good feeling about this.

He snatched up his desk phone and called Nash. He told him what he'd discovered. "Richardson could be there. We need to check out Clyde's place."

"He could be a hostage," Nash said. "I still have two police officers at Richardson's house. I'll let them know and see if they remembered Clyde's car leaving yesterday or coming back to his place."

"Let's meet down at the end of the block where the road curves. Clyde's home sits back from the houses around it. We might be able to use that to our advantage. We'll have to be careful. I could see Richardson killing Clyde if we hit the place hard and heavy."

"Agreed. I'll be there in twenty minutes. Tell the police officers to be circumspect. We don't want Richardson to get suspicious, if he's there."

"They can be our eyes. See you soon."

Taylor ended the call and quickly left his office. As he got into his SUV, returned to him after being fixed, he punched in Dallas's number. "We have a lead on Richardson." He filled in his fellow Texas Ranger about the neighbor.

"I'll let Sierra know."

"How is she? Has the doctor come by yet?"

"She's okay, but the doctor is running late. It won't be for a while. She's resting right now. She asked about you."

She's in the hospital because I couldn't stop her from getting hurt again.

He swallowed down the guilt. "I'll let you know what happens." Taylor ended the call and started his car, more determined than ever to end this today.

He arrived at the meeting place before Nash and called his dad. "How's Ben doing?"

"He drew a picture of you and Sierra, then he wrote a big question mark. I told him you and Sierra were working together and would be back soon. I've been keeping him busy trying to teach his puppy tricks."

"He's talking?"

"No, I'm giving the commands. I almost thought he would say something, but he didn't."

Nash pulled up behind Taylor. "I've got to go, Dad. Bye."

Taylor exited the car, picturing Ben trying to train his puppy. He smiled. He could remember TJ, on one of his good days, doing the same thing with Oscar.

"My guys at Richardson's house confirmed that a car in Zoller's garage left yesterday before the shooting. It never came back."

Taylor frowned. He didn't have a good feeling about this. "How many were in the car?"

"One. An older man."

"Which could fit Richardson in the disguise he used at the shooting."

"I have a bomb dog coming. If we go inside, Zoller's house needs to be checked for explosives. We don't know what Richardson is up to."

"He could have left the area. I sent the disguise and car he was driving yesterday to SAPD headquarters. Your captain is getting it out to all law enforcement agencies as well as the media. Maybe someone has spotted him." Taylor went to the back of his SUV and removed his bullet-proof vest and put it on while Nash did the same thing. "We'll need at least one officer at Richardson's house to cover the back of Zoller's."

"I've got more backup coming. It should be here soon with our K-9 officer." Nash unfolded a detailed map of the area. "Love satellite imagery."

Patience was important when planning a raid on a place, but it was hard for Taylor to restrain his urge to charge up to the house and see if Richardson was inside. He couldn't shake the feeling that the killer was planning something else. If only he'd known that Richardson most likely was in the house when Clyde opened the door. This could have ended days ago. Instead Sierra was in the hospital and the killer, who was a gifted makeup artist when he went to college, was roaming around somewhere possibly trying to figure out how to get to someone else who he thought had crossed him.

It seemed an eternity later that the rest of the officers arrived. The sight of the team converging on him and Nash calmed Taylor. He had to be calm in order to do his job. He had to put everything else out of his mind but the mission. Even if Richardson wasn't there, Clyde could be, along with some clue to where the killer was going next.

Please, God, let Clyde be alive. Let no one else be harmed by Richardson.

As Nash filled in the officers, Taylor called Nanny Bee's number. He had one more thing to check. When she answered, he said, "Ms. Bee, I'm the Texas Ranger who came by and talked to you a couple of days before about Max Richardson. Have you seen him since then?"

"No."

"Have you seen anything unusual at Clyde Zoller's house in the past two days?"

"This morning I didn't see him drinking his coffee on his porch."

"But he did Sunday and Saturday?"

"I don't know. I sleep late on the weekend. Is that all? I've got a show I want to watch."

"I appreciate your help. I just need to tell you

the police and I will be crossing your backyard. Stay in the house, on the far side, until a police officer tells you it's okay."

"I…" Her voice faded.

"Ms. Bee?"

"What's going on?"

"We believe Clyde is in danger, and we don't want anything happening to you." Taylor glanced at Nash, who tapped the face of his watch. Taylor held up his palm.

"Does this have anything to do with Max Richardson?"

He started to say he wasn't at liberty to tell her, but he nixed that. "Yes," he said before he disconnected the call.

As he led the officers, they remained stealthy so as not to alert their shooter. As before at Richardson's house, Taylor, Nash, the police officer with the battering ram and the K-9 handler with his bomb-sniffing dog went to the front of Clyde's place while the last two covered the back exit. After the German shepherd checked the entrance for possible explosives, it took two strikes with the ram to burst open the door. The K-9 team went in first, heading toward the left. Taylor and the rest followed.

Three steps into the living room he came to

an abrupt stop. His gaze fixed on Clyde Zoller tied to a chair, his head dropped forward.

Sierra lay on her hospital bed, eyes closed. Her whole body ached, as though a herd of cattle trampled over her. Anxiety filled her. She wanted to be home. She wanted her life back. And she wanted to remember what she was forgetting.

Something nagged at her, vague and indistinct, and try as she might to bring the memory into focus, she couldn't. Going back through all the patient files in her mind didn't give her the answer to the question that had been pestering her since she woke up this morning.

Her hands grabbed the bed sheet and fisted around the cotton, the muscles in her arms tightening, causing pain to radiate from her wound. She relaxed the tension in her body and took in deep, calming breaths. Forcing herself to remember wasn't helping her.

The door swished open. She opened her eyes to see Dallas returning to her room after checking in with the police officer relieving the previous guard. "When is the doctor coming?" she asked him.

"He's running late. The nurse said probably another hour or so."

"I need to get home to Ben. This has to affect his recovery."

"John's at the house. And Robert said the puppy is really helping to take Ben's mind off what's going on."

"I need to hold Ben. I need to see he's all right." *And Taylor.*

"I know what you mean. I feel that way about my daughter, Michelle, and my soon-to-be one. When Katie was stolen, I did anything I could to bring her home safely. With Taylor's help I did bring her back to Rachel. She isn't my daughter biologically, but I love her as much as Michelle."

"That's how I feel about Ben. He's everything to me. And there's nothing I can do to help him. He's so afraid he isn't talking, a kid who loved to talk. How are we going to get through this?"

"One day at a time. Not always easy to do."

"Have you heard anything from Taylor? What if something happened when they went back to the neighbor across the street? I don't want anyone else to end up here in the hospi—" Sierra snapped her fingers. "I remember!"

"What?"

"I've been racking my memory to come up with something I read in Richardson's daughter's file ever since I was brought in last night. At first, I thought maybe his daughter was brought here that last time when she died, and that consequence bothered me yesterday. But it wasn't this hospital. Now I remember this is the same place where the trial treatment she didn't qualify for is being run. If Richardson has another target, I would say this hospital is it."

"And you are here, too." Dallas frowned and pulled out his cell phone. "I'm calling Taylor to let him know."

Sierra needed to get out of here. She sat straight up and swung her legs over the side of the bed but paused when she spied Dallas's deepening scowl. "What's wrong?"

"Taylor isn't answering his cell phone."

TWELVE

Taylor hurried to Clyde and put his fingers against his neck. When he found a pulse, he untied the gag around his mouth and shook the older man while scanning his body for any wounds. "Call 911."

Clyde rallied, his eyes saucer round when he looked into Taylor's face. The neighbor blinked and panned the living room full of law enforcement officers. "Where's Richardson?"

"That's what I want to know." Taylor began untying the ropes around his chest, arms and legs while the rest of the officers searched the premises.

Clyde stared at the curtains over the window, a slit of light peeking through. "What time is it?"

"Twelve noon. How long have you been tied up?"

"I don't know."

Taylor released the last rope around the older man and stood. "Was Richardson in your house when I came by to see you on Friday afternoon?"

Clyde nodded. "I tried to tell you, but with Max right next to me and his gun pointing at me, I couldn't say anything to alert you that something was wrong. The only thing I could say was Nanny Bee was a nice lady. As you no doubt found out, she isn't."

Taylor berated himself for missing that clue. He should have realized the cranky, self-absorbed woman he met was different from the talkative, friendly neighbor Clyde had described.

Nash returned to the living room. "His car isn't in the garage."

"Tell me what happened." Taylor offered Clyde a hand and helped him stand.

Clyde wobbled and held on to Taylor. "I'm used to walking as much as I can to keep these legs moving."

Taylor saw his cane on the floor nearby, grabbed it and handed it to Clyde.

He walked a few steps, then turned toward Taylor. "He made himself up to look like me, so he could leave here undetected. He even took one of my canes. I saw what he had in his duffel bag. Several guns and what looked like a bomb about the size of a shoe box. I asked him what he was going to do with that. He told me to shut up."

"Just one bomb?" Nash asked.

"Yes. Max didn't say much, but after he tied me up and took my car keys, he looked me in the eye and said he was going to settle a score. 'They can't walk around while my Charlie is dead.' Those were his exact words. Then he left. I knew he wasn't coming back. I could read it in his eyes. After he left, the first few hours I struggled to get loose. Finally, exhaustion took over, and I left it in the Lord's hands and look, y'all showed up."

"Did he talk about where he was going? Like the River Walk or a funeral?"

"No," Clyde said when the paramedics showed up.

While the EMTs were checking to make sure Clyde was all right, Taylor stepped out onto the porch with Nash. "So now we know there's another target. We've got to figure where he's striking next."

"Do you think Sierra might know a connection concerning Richardson's daughter?"

Taylor pulled out his cell phone. "I'll get in touch with Dallas. You alert the police." When he looked at his screen, he noticed a missed call from his friend. He punched the button to return the call. "Sorry. I was in the middle of a raid on Richardson's neighbor." He'd silenced his phone so if it rang the sound wouldn't give him away. He quickly filled Dallas in on what they discovered.

"Sierra thinks she knows where Richardson is going next. Lone Star Hospital. It's where the drug trial is taking place that his daughter didn't get into."

"Sierra needs to get out of there now. I'm on my way. Nash is letting his superiors know about the risk. The hospital will be locked down, but we may be too late. He could already be inside." After Taylor disconnected with Dallas, he filled in Nash, who was already on the phone with SAPD headquarters.

The K-9 officer and his dog were right behind them, but more than one would be needed to cover the whole hospital. Nash requested more for the hospital.

They were fifteen minutes away, and to Taylor that seemed as though it was clear across Texas.

"What's wrong?" Sierra stood next to the bed, holding on to it to keep her balance. For a few seconds light-headedness made her unsteady.

Dallas told her what Taylor had said to him. "There's a good chance Richardson will come to the hospital or is already here."

"He's going to set off another bomb?" She remembered the last time she'd been at the clinic when one had exploded. Now she was on the third floor and outrunning an explosion was highly unlikely, especially with her equilibrium being off.

"He had a duffel bag with several guns and a bomb in it when he left Clyde's house yesterday. In spite of two bomb threats at the hotel and funeral home, we didn't find one, so he must still have it with him."

"To use at the hospital." Sierra gathered her clothes and made her way toward the bathroom as quickly as she could.

"I'm sure there are security guards now at each entrance."

"Then I'll pray he isn't inside." Sierra hurried as fast as she could, considering her aches, bruises and bandaged arm restricted any quick movements. She caught a look at herself in the mirror. The woman who stared back at her had a big goose egg on her forehead above her right eyebrow where she hit the cement. Dark circles under her eyes added to her haggard look.

Lord, I'm in Your hands. Ben needs me.

Please get me out of here safely. He's already lost his mother. Protect everyone here, especially Taylor. Help the police find Max Richardson before he kills again.

When she exited the bathroom, Dallas was already standing by the door into the hallway. She knew that Dallas was Taylor's friend and he would protect her, but she wished Taylor was here. She always felt safe around him, even when they were running out of the clinic right before the bomb went off.

As she and Dallas left the room, the officer standing guard, who'd introduced himself as Officer Bailey, followed behind them. She knew he had seen a photo of what Richardson looked like without his disguise and how he'd looked yesterday. But Richardson most likely was masquerading as someone different today, and Taylor told her how he was studying the shooter's mannerism and the way he walked.

"Ms. Walker, where are you going?" a nurse asked at the counter they passed.

"Home."

"But the doctor hasn't signed the release papers."

"If I have a problem, I'll go to my physician. Thanks for taking such good care of me." Sierra began moving toward the elevator, slower than she would have liked.

Dallas punched the lobby button while Sierra and Officer Bailey entered and leaned against the wall. As the elevator opened on the second floor, and a couple with a young girl entered, the alarm system went off followed by an announcement to evacuate the building immediately. Dallas held the door open to allow as many people as they could into the elevator before it continued its descent.

Sierra studied the faces of everyone around her. She would never feel safe until the shooter was captured. She told herself her nemesis wasn't interested in her but was probably heading for the area where the medical trial was being conducted.

The doors opened, and everyone flooded out into the lobby. Sierra, Dallas and Officer Bailey waited until the elevator was cleared, then left. People jammed the lobby as they funneled toward the front entrance. A big man jostled against her. Dallas and her police guard crowded closer, forming a barrier between her and the others trying to leave. In the mob Richardson could be anywhere. The thought sent her heart racing twice as fast.

* * *

While staff, visitors and patients were being evacuated from the hospital, Taylor, Nash and the K-9 officer with his dog pushed their way through the throng toward the first-floor labs where the bomb most likely would be planted. Taylor wished he knew how big the bomb was in Richardson's duffel bag. They joined other SAPD officers with three K-9 teams starting with the rooms that were part of the medical trial. Taylor accompanied a canine team assigned to search the office of the head of the study. If he were Richardson, he would go after the person who made the decisions about who participated in the drug trial.

When the German shepherd sniffed a cabinet, he sat and barked. The bomb squad took over going through their protocol.

While they carefully opened the door, Taylor stood back and breathed a sigh of relief when no tripwires set off an explosion. He moved closer and glimpsed the bomb, similar in size to the one he remembered at the clinic. "Is it activated?" he asked the officer.

"Yes. We have five minutes to disarm it. I think I can, but get everyone out of here in case I'm wrong."

Taylor spun around and raced out into the

hall. "There's a bomb. Leave," he told the officers and medical personnel.

The head of the bomb squad approached him. "That includes you. Make sure this whole area is evacuated and get out."

While Taylor made his way toward the main lobby, he checked every room along the way. If the explosion was like the one at the clinic, it would take out a portion of the first floor, which could affect the basement and the other levels above.

In the hospital lobby, there was a bank of four doors people were trying to move through to get outside. He searched the crowd for Dallas wearing his cowboy hat. Being tall, he would stand above a lot of the others. Taylor spied him toward the front and weaved his way in that direction.

His cell phone rang. It was the bomb squad commander. Taylor quickly answered it. "Was it defused?"

"Yes. We want the evacuation to continue until we have scoured the whole building and checked security tapes."

"I'll do that. The security office isn't far from me. I was able to ID Richardson in disguise at the shooting yesterday. I might be able to again."

"Good. Keep me informed."

Taylor glanced back at where Dallas stood with Sierra and a police officer. They were almost outside. As he made his way to the security office, fighting against the flow of people, he called Dallas. "The bomb has been defused, but the commander wants to make sure that's all. I'm checking security tapes of the area where the bomb was. Get Sierra to a safe place. Remember, Richardson shot her when she left the funeral home, so be on alert."

"You think he's hanging around to see what happened?"

"He did at the funeral home. And after the clinic was blown up, he went to the crime scene, so yes, I do."

"There'll be a command center set up outside. She'll be safe there."

"Thanks." Taylor tried to open the door to the security office, but it was locked. He knocked, waited half a minute and then dug into his pocket for his case with various picks.

The door swung wide. A security guard stood in the entrance. "You must be Texas Ranger Blackburn. The commander called to tell me to pull up the footage from the lab section and offices behind the bank of main elevators on the first floor. I only arrived back in here a minute ago. I was told to evacuate, too."

"Let's run it in slow motion backward. It would be faster that way because I don't have any idea when the bomb was planted in the director of special projects' office."

"I have a camera that'll show the hallway in front of his office. Nothing inside."

"Good. That's all I need. I didn't see another way into the office." Taylor took a seat next to the security guard and began viewing the footage.

A lot of people went up and down that hall but no one went into the room where the bomb was found. Then Taylor saw a police officer with a backpack walking backward to the door. Then he ducked inside after looking up and down the corridor. Taylor sat forward. "That must be Richardson." He watched the video going backward, then said, "Now play it forward in regular time." He needed to be sure it was Richardson in makeup that made him look younger and his upper-body physique more muscular. He had his police hat on, so he couldn't see all his face clearly, but he didn't have to. He favored the same leg as Richardson did. His walk was the same as he followed the progression of the officer to the elevator and saw that he went to Sierra's floor. He'd gone after Sierra, staying in the hospital, even with the bomb going off.

Granted, her room was at the other end of the building where he placed it, but he was taking a chance the explosion wouldn't harm that part. Then in the confusion of leaving the hospital, he would kill her.

Taylor noted the time stamp on the screen and realized that was the time that the police guard at Sierra's door would change. Was Richardson with Dallas and Sierra right now? His heart racing, Taylor fumbled for his cell phone as he charged out of the security office.

Guarded by Dallas and Officer Bailey, Sierra approached the police mobile command post, a white truck with a black-and-gold stripe. Pain thumped against the side of her head. Even being in bed for the past eighteen hours, exhaustion encompassed her whole body. "Instead of going inside there, can I go home to Ben? That way I won't be here for the shooter to come after me. There are two police officers at the house."

"My patrol car isn't too far away. I could drive her, sir, if she wants to go."

Sierra looked at Officer Bailey, then Dallas. Everything that had happened the past week was catching up with her. "Please." She didn't want to be another target for Richardson.

Dallas nodded. "But I'll need to let Taylor

know, and I'll come with you. You can't have too many guards."

Officer Bailey pointed to his police cruiser several rows away.

Sierra headed that way with Dallas on one side while Bailey was on her left slightly behind her. She scanned the parking lot, then kept focused on the vehicle that would take her away from the chaos all around her.

Dallas's cell phone rang as Officer Bailey opened the back door for Sierra. Dallas stepped away to answer the call while she slid into the car and reclined her head back against the cushion. She just wanted the pounding to go away.

"The police officer with you is Richardson," Taylor said into his phone while moving through the crowd as quickly as he could. He kept the mobile command post in his sight.

"We were leaving to go to your—"

"Dallas?"

A sound like his friend had dropped his cell phone filled Taylor's ear. He swept the parking lot around the command post and spied a police officer scurrying around a vehicle and hopping into the front. Richardson.

Taylor hurried through the crowd as he made another call, this time to the police chief. He explained what was going down as the cruiser pulled out of the parking space. Taylor was still three rows away, but he pumped every ounce of energy into his legs.

"Hurry. Set up a barricade." Taylor clutched his cell phone in his fist as he arrived at where the car had been.

Dallas lay on the concrete, facedown. *Please be alive.*

Taylor knelt next to his friend, feeling for a pulse. "Officer down in row twelve," he told the chief on the phone. "He's alive, but Richardson has driven off toward the northwest exit with Sierra Walker." He stood and waved so the police could see where he was.

Once he got their attention, he swung around and followed Richardson's flight.

If Richardson kills Sierra... Taylor couldn't complete the thought. The prospect of losing her threatened his ability to stop Richardson.

And right now he could let nothing stop him from saving Sierra.

Sierra's heavy eyelids slid open when the police cruiser came to an abrupt halt, throwing her forward. Where was Dallas? She glanced out the window. Cops were all around the vehicle with guns pointed at them. What was going on?

A voice over a loudspeaker said, "Surrender now. If you make a move with that gun, we'll consider you hostile and return fire. Put your hands behind your head and step out of the vehicle. Now."

"What's happening?" Sierra asked, the quaver in her voice making her words barely above a whisper.

Leaning forward, she saw from the side Officer Bailey's jaw clench, a tic twitching his cheek. And then it hit her.

"Are you Max Richardson?"

"You deserve to die."

Fear rippled down her length, but she tried to hold it together. "No amount of deaths will bring your daughter back. I fought the insurance company for Charlene. It was too late to help her."

"Shut up! No one cared about her. They killed my wife, too."

A movement out of the corner of her eye caught Sierra's attention. Taylor joined the other officers, his gun pointed at Richardson.

"My sister cared. She tried to convince the doctor in charge of the study, and you killed her. Now my nephew has only me to raise him. He had nothing to do with this situation, and yet he lost his mother and now you want to kill me."

"I have nothing to lose now. I'm a dead man. I might as well settle the score."

Death by cop. But not before he kills me. What do I say to that?

Words flooded her mind. "Max, don't you want to see your little girl again? You will if you believe in the Lord."

"He took my Charlie. It's too late for me," Richardson yelled, staring at the police around them.

Tears blurred her vision. "It's never too—"

Suddenly he lifted his gun and shot himself in the head as Sierra threw herself onto the floor, expecting a barrage of bullets to hit the car.

The sound of the driver's door opening reverberated through the vehicle. Slowly Sierra lifted her head and scrambled out of the back seat.

Right into Taylor's arms.

It was dark when Sierra entered Robert's house. Taylor was right behind her, strangely quiet most of the ride there.

One glance over her shoulder at Taylor and she knew something was wrong. But what? Richardson was dead, and he couldn't hurt anyone else.

When they entered the living room Ben looked up, saw her and ran to her, throwing his arms around her and hugging her tightly. She knelt and pulled him against her chest. "I love you, Ben. We can go home tomorrow. Everything is safe again."

Her nephew didn't say anything but remained clinging to her. Sierra stayed in place until Ben finally released her and held her hand to walk her deeper into the living room. The sight of the lit Christmas tree gave her a calmness she hadn't had for hours—since she'd tried to talk the shooter into surrendering. Instead, he killed himself, dying with no reconciliation with God. Saddened by that fact, she found herself forgiving the man. She wouldn't let hatred bring her down. The following months would be hard enough without carrying around a deep loathing for the man who had changed her and Ben's lives forever.

When Sierra sat on the couch, Ben picked up his puppy and immediately sat beside her. Ben was safe now. *Thank You, God.*

Taylor stood next to the Christmas tree, tense, a serious expression on his face. "I can't stay. I need to go to the police station to take care of some of the necessary reports."

"When will you be back?" Robert asked before Sierra could.

He shrugged. "I also need to check on Dallas. He says he's all right, but he has said that before and hasn't been."

"Take my word. He has a whopping headache." Sierra hugged Ben closer. "But time will take care of that. Tell him thanks again from me."

"I will." Taylor crossed to the front door and left.

Silence filled the room for several minutes until Ben's puppy began to whine.

Robert rose. "That's his sign he wants to go outside. I need to take Oscar. I'll take him, too. You want to come, Ben?"

He handed his puppy to Robert but remained next to Sierra's side. When Taylor's father left with the dogs, she kissed the top of Ben's head. "You know that we're safe now. When we return to our house tomorrow, we only have one week until Christmas. We're going to have a lot to clean and do." She'd started to tell him about Richardson destroying their Christmas decorations and ornaments. She couldn't right now. She didn't want him to fear his home because Richardson had been in there. He had enough to deal with. He still wasn't talking.

When Robert returned with the two dogs, Sierra pushed to her feet. "It's past your bedtime," she told her nephew. "Let's get ready."

After Ben put on his pajamas, he brushed his teeth and knelt by the bed. He bowed his head while Sierra asked God to watch out for the people they loved and thanked Him for taking care of them. She yearned for the time when her nephew would say his prayers aloud. The silence made her throat ache with sorrow.

She tucked him in, and then Oscar lay on his right side while the puppy cuddled next to Ben on the other one. Just for tonight she'd let the pup stay there, out of the crate. She kissed Ben's forehead and said, "Good night."

She left, leaving the door open slightly, and made her way down the stairs to the kitchen. She needed a drink of water and some advice from Robert. After filling a glass, she went into the living room and took a seat across from Taylor's dad. "Tonight, all I could say to Ben about when we go home is that we'll need to clean the house. I couldn't tell him about the destroyed decorations. I don't want him to be afraid of our house."

"I've called a couple of guys I know from church who have agreed to help me clean your place tomorrow morning. I'll pick up a tree on the way and some ornaments."

"But he'll know it isn't our tree."

"I know. Being told that it was knocked down

and seeing the damage is two different things. He doesn't need to know all the gritty details. When he comes into the house, he won't see the destruction."

"What if he asks about it?"

"If he does, that means he's talking. That's a good sign. Tell him the truth in broad terms and let him know you're there for him. You know, I'm going to miss Ben. My daughter's family is sharing the holidays with her husband's family in Oregon. It's going to be lonely around here. I hope y'all will come here on Christmas and enjoy a meal and time with us."

Us. Meaning Robert and Taylor. "I'd love to see you, but you need to check with your son. Today Taylor has been—" she searched for a word to describe her gut feeling about him "—distant."

"How do you feel about Taylor?"

"I care about him—a lot."

"For the past week you've worked intensely together on the case. You two have gone through an emotional ride in a short time that many don't experience over years." Robert stared at the floor between them for a moment, then lifted his head and looked into her eyes. "Seeing Ben and Taylor together reminded me of my son with TJ. I never thought I would see that again. He took TJ's death very hard. But with you he's let down his guard. I imagine when he was running after the car Richardson was driving with you in it, he was scared. That man had hurt you twice already."

"I'm fine. I survived because he discovered Officer Bailey was Richardson."

Robert nodded. "But your wounds are still very evident every time he looks at you. Knowing my son, he blames himself for that. He didn't protect you enough. You see, when his wife died, he felt he should have done something to save her, but then he didn't have much time to grieve because he had to raise a baby and deal with a new job that he'd wanted his whole life."

"Being a Texas Ranger?"

"Yes. That's all he talked about when he was a kid. Give him time. I know he cares about you."

As she rose, so did Robert. "Thanks for the advice and for cleaning the house tomorrow. I don't know what Ben and I would have done without Taylor and you." She covered the distance to Robert and kissed him on the cheek. "I'm going to turn in. See you in the morning."

"You might not see me in the morning. I'll

be leaving early for your house. I'll get the key to your place from Taylor."

She smiled and headed for the staircase. As she mounted the steps, she thanked God for all the people saved today, especially the real Officer Bailey, who had been knocked out and tied up, and Clyde Zoller. She was also grateful that the bomb hadn't exploded, or else the number of victims could have been high.

She checked on Ben, then entered her room and sat on the bed. Her thoughts turned to Taylor and what his father had said. *I know he cares about you.*

She more than cared about Taylor.

I love him. What am I going to do?

Taylor had avoided Sierra as much as possible the past day by keeping busy wrapping up all the loose ends with the case. But now he was picking them up at his dad's house and driving them to their home. When he went into the kitchen, he nearly collided with Sierra coming out of the room. Their gazes embraced, and for the life of him, he couldn't look away. Her bruises and cuts stood out even more, shouting to the world what she'd gone through.

If he had found out about Officer Bailey a few minutes later than he had, Sierra would have been murdered by Richardson. And he would be mourning another person he cared about. No, he more than cared about her—and that was the problem.

He finally blinked and glanced away. "Are you two ready? Dad has everything cleaned up and an extra surprise for Ben."

"What?"

"He wouldn't tell me. He likes to surprise people."

"We're ready. Ben is outside playing with Oscar and his puppy. He's going to miss Oscar."

And I'm going to miss you and Ben. If only I could control the future. But I can't.

"I'll go get Ben. Our stuff is by the front door."

While she walked out to the backyard, Taylor stared at the coffeepot for a long moment until he heard them come into the house. He quickly filled a travel mug and followed them into the entry hall. Silence filled the car as he drove toward their home.

He pulled into their driveway and carried their bags toward the house. His dad waited at the door and stood to the side to let them in.

When Ben strolled into the living room, his eyes grew huge. It looked like a Christmas store, with a huge colorful tree, decorations everywhere and even a banner hanging across the dining room entrance that said, "Merry Christmas to Ben and Sierra."

Taylor noticed some similar holiday decorations from the first time he'd been in this house. "Ben, this would be a good time to put the ornaments you made on your tree." He handed the child the box they had collected at the clinic after the bombing, with four handmade ornaments in it.

While Ben was deciding where to hang them, Sierra looked from his father to Taylor. Tears glistened in her eyes. "You both went above and beyond. Thank you."

His dad bridged the distance between them and said, "I've also stocked your refrigerator."

Sierra hugged him. "It's only fair both of you come for Christmas dinner next week."

"But I already invited y'all to my place."

"Please let me do this for you both. Words can't express my gratitude."

"Then I'll be here on Christmas. Right now I need to go to a meeting at church." Robert turned toward Ben. "I'll see you later and help you with training your puppy."

Ben waved goodbye with a big smile on his face.

"How's Dallas doing?" Sierra asked Taylor after his father had left.

Taylor leaned close and whispered, "Not happy he didn't figure out who the officer was. I told him next time." When he pulled back, the whiff of vanilla she wore still filled his nostrils.

Taylor put the last of the bags on the floor. "I'd better leave, too."

"Do you have to?"

"I still have a report to finish." Which was true, but that wasn't why he wanted to put some distance between them. Being with her and realizing how close she'd come to dying caused his heart to ache.

Sierra didn't say anything else.

"Ben, I'm going. Let me know when you figure out a name for your puppy. Bye." Taylor turned to leave. When he clasped the doorknob, the little boy, holding his dog, came into the entry hall, standing next to Sierra. "See you two." Taylor opened the door.

"His name is Buddy. Don't go."

Ben's voice halted Taylor in midstride. He faced the child, then looked at Sierra.

"Stay and have dinner with us." Her warm expression tore down all his barriers. "We need to celebrate Ben talking."

Taylor couldn't refuse her—or Ben. "Only

if you let me order pizza. And I agree. Tonight we celebrate."

She drew him toward her and smiled. "Perfect."

Taylor leaned forward and kissed her with all the love he felt for her.

With Buddy in one arm, Ben threw his other around Taylor. "I love pizza."

Taylor tousled his hair. "I know. Are you ready to celebrate?"

"Yes!" Ben pumped his arm into the air then pushed Taylor nearer to Sierra. "All together."

EPILOGUE

Christmas Eve one year later

Sierra stood at the stove stirring the Blackburn family hot chocolate recipe that Robert had shared with her. Suddenly she sensed someone behind her and knew who it was. "I should get you that bell from the Christmas tree to keep you from sneaking up on me."

Chuckling, Taylor leaned close and nibbled the side of her neck. "Mmm. You smell wonderful."

"I added vanilla to the hot chocolate. You know how I love vanilla. I hope your dad doesn't mind."

Taylor came around beside her at the stove. "How are you feeling?"

"Fine, if your daughter would quit practicing her gymnastics when I'm trying to take a nap."

He laid his hand on Sierra's belly. "It won't be too much longer, sweetie. You'll be here soon enough. Your mother needs her rest." He bent over and kissed her stomach.

Sierra turned off the burner. "This is ready to serve."

Taylor slid his arms around her and pulled her close. "I love you, Mrs. Blackburn. More every day I'm with you."

"I love you, too. I never thought I would ever find someone like you. You are my hero in every sense of the word." She drew his head down and kissed him with all the love she had for him.

"Aunt Sierra, where is the hot chocolate? We've been waiting forever."

Sierra looked around Taylor at Ben standing in the doorway from the dining room, grinning at catching them kissing. "We're coming. Remember, you can only open one present on Christmas Eve."

Ben whirled around and darted away.

Taylor touched her forehead with his. "The best decision I ever made was staying that night Ben asked me to. It took a while for me to realize that we have to turn control over to the Lord and enjoy the good moments and endure the bad ones. Worrying about what might happen in the future only holds us back, and every day I've been with you that has been reinforced."

"And I've been on the same journey as you. Embrace the moment."

Taylor drew her even closer and kissed her, declaring his love.

"Aunt Sierra," Ben yelled from the living room.

Sierra reluctantly pulled away and poured the hot chocolate into the mugs on the tray. "I have no idea where Ben gets his impatience."

Taylor laughed. "This from a woman who wants her baby born months ago so she can hold her."

Sierra entered the living room first with Taylor right behind her. While he placed the tray on the coffee table, she stood back, taking in the scene before her. Ben sat on the floor by the Christmas tree with Buddy on one side and Oscar on the other. Robert sat on the couch, and John occupied a lounge chair near Ben. Her nephew still saw John but only once a month. It had taken a team—her, Taylor, John, Robert, Buddy and Oscar—to help Ben deal with the trauma of his mother's death. He no longer had nightmares or periods of silence. This year he had been right in the middle of decorating the

Christmas tree and even made a few more ornaments for it.

Ben grabbed something from under the tree and crossed the room to Sierra. "This is for little Kathleen. Since she can't open the gift yet, I thought you would."

Sierra took the wrapped present and opened it. It was a three-dimensional ornament of the baby Jesus in a manger. Tears blurred her vision. Smiling, she gave Ben a hug, then handed the ornament to him. "Please put it on the tree for Kathleen."

While her nephew studied the pine for a special place for the manger, Taylor wrapped his arms around Sierra from behind her and whispered, "Kathleen couldn't have a better big brother than him."

When Ben hung the decoration, Sierra leaned back against Taylor, relishing the safety and love she experienced being in her husband's embrace.

* * * * *

*If you loved this exciting romantic suspense,
pick up the other books in Margaret Daley's
Lone Star Justice miniseries*

High Risk Reunion
Lone Star Christmas Rescue
Texas Ranger Showdown
Texas Baby Pursuit

Available now from Love Inspired Suspense!

*Find more great reads at
www.LoveInspired.com.*

Dear Reader,

Lone Star Christmas Witness is my fifth book in the Lone Star Justice series, about Texas Rangers. In this story, a tragedy happens that changes my heroine's life. Not only does she have to deal with her own grief, but also try to help her nephew who lost the only parent he's known.

This is a story of how people handle grief. The little boy who loses his mother stops talking and withdraws. The heroine is trying to stay alive and protect her nephew while also dealing with the sudden death of her older sister, who had been more of a mother to her than a sister. Their worlds are forever changed. Not only are they affected, but the Texas Ranger dealing with the case has to finally come to terms with the death of his son several years before who was about the age of the little boy he is trying to keep alive. You can try to suppress pain, but sooner or later it bubbles up to the surface and has to be dealt with.

I love hearing from readers. You can contact me at margaretdaley@gmail.com or at PO box 2074, Tulsa, OK 74101. You can also learn more about my books at www.margaretdaley.

com. I have a newsletter that you can sign up for on my website.

Best wishes,

Margaret Daley